NETTLEWORTH PARVA

NETTLEWORTH PARVA

by

Fred Kitchen

LONDON
J. M. DENT & SONS LTD

Contents

CHAPTER ONE

The Deserted Village

It was said of Nettleworth Parva that it was a place where
nothing ever happened. But then it contained so few inhabitants,
just a cluster of cottages and three farmsteads. It had not even a
village inn to cause a little stir among the community on Saturday
nights. The village (if it could be called a village) depended for
its entertainment on its bigger brother Nettleworth Magna,
which while of no great size itself was quite a flourishing place
compared to Parva. The little colony, commonly known as
Parva to distinguish it from the larger unit of Magna, nestled at
the foot of Magna hill on a narrow lane leading to the main road
to Kingsmill. It was a charming and secluded little spot, well
away from the busy throng of life, whose vocation was mainly
agriculture with a few hands employed at the nearby stone
quarries. One other man gainfully employed was the roadman
Joe Wrigley, who in rainy weather collected white lime-like
sludge off the roads and in summer swept dust several inches
thick into the gutter; with very little effect, for in winter the
carriages were bespattered with a thick coating of limewash,
while the cyclist ended his journey with his back sprayed with the
same material, and in summer the traffic rode through a cloud of
dust that whitened the wayside hedges with lime. The main
roads were not in quite so parlous a state, being made and mended
with ganister, a granite-like bluish stone that did not grind into
powder so quickly as the local limestone used on the by-roads.

One day in the summer of 1904 Joe Wrigley was following his
lawful occupation of sweeping the one street that meandered
through the little hamlet of Nettleworth when a motor-car drew
up. Though motors were becoming fairly common in the district,

a motor in the street of Parva was such a rarity that Joe decided to investigate. The occupants, a man and a woman, had alighted and were obviously enjoying the scenery. A cart track branched off from the foot of Magna hill down to the water-mill where the bank of the dam and the stream were a blaze of golden kingcups. From there a long stretch of pasture on which cattle were grazing reached up to the roadway, making as pleasing a picture as anyone could wish to see. Joe Wrigley, a chubby, red-faced fellow in corded trousers strapped at the knee, and wearing a blue smock, drew near and set down his wheelbarrow. He leaned on his brush handle for a while in contemplative silence, some might have said with a vacant look, though there was nothing vacant about Joe; his silence merely expressed the fact of his living in a place where nothing ever happened, a place where time stood still.

Presently he spat in his wheelbarrow, and remarked: 'Yer can't leave yer motor-car theer, mister.'

The man turned on being addressed and recrossed the road. He was a dapper little man, neatly dressed in a pin-striped suit with buttoned boots of patent leather; but most noticeable was his neatly waxed moustache which he habitually twisted in his thumb and finger as a spare-time occupation.

'Is my car in your way, my man?' he asked as he drew near.

''Taint me, mister,' was the reply; 'the lad's fetching t' cows up and yer've left yer car in't gate hoil,' indicating where a herd of milk cows were approaching out of the fields they had been so intently admiring.

The man moved his car out of the gateway, and he and his wife stayed to watch the rustic scene of a small boy driving home a dozen head of dairy cows for milking time. He was a bright-looking boy in spite of a portion of his trouser seat having failed to conceal his shirt lap, while his shoes revealed his bare toes. He gave the strangers and their car a prolonged and quizzical stare, as though such things were out of the ordinary in his young life, then followed his herd through the gateway, clinging to the last one's tail.

'Come along, Quiddy boy,' called the roadman as the boy passed through the gateway, 'thou'rt too slow to fetch cows up.' At which the boy grinned and remarked: 'Gaffer Western'll twank my starn if he sees me hurrying his milk cows.'

The roadway being now clear of its bovine traffic, though it took full five minutes for the small herd of cows to pass through the gateway, such was the pace of life in Parva, the stranger inquired: 'What is the name of this place, my good fellow?'

To which Joe replied: 'This be Nettleworth Parva, sir, and yon be Nettleworth Magna,' pointing his brush handle up the hill.

'What a charming little place, so quiet and restful,' remarked the lady, joining in.

'Aye, it ain't amiss for them as likes it so,' responded the roadman, 'but it's a dead-alive hole in a manner o' speaking, missis. There's nowt i' Parva—why, if a fellar wants to wet his whistle he mu' thoil up that hill to Magna. There's nowt to be getten here but sarasperella and sich, or a bit o' bacca at Mrs Humble's which is like smoking clover knobs sho's had it drying in the shop owerlong.'

'Yes,' agreed the lady, 'it is a disadvantage being so remote from the shops, but a charming place none the less.'

The roadman seemed inclined for a chat, which was not surprising in that deserted spot, and after again spitting into his wheelbarrow said: 'They do say as how the houses in Parva were built o' the stoans intended for Nettleworth Magna from the quarries back yonder, and when the carters came to the foot o' Magna hill they would throw off a few gurt stoans to ease their 'osses. Seem'ly they never bothered to pick 'em up agin, and there they ligged till somebody thought to build hissel a house where all these loose stoans lay ready to hand. That started it, and first one and then another started to build until all the loose stoans were cleared up which, they say, is why Parva is nobbut half finished.'

Such was the roadman's account of the founding of Nettleworth Parva. The stranger then inquired if it were possible to procure a cup of tea in the place called Magna, explaining they were somewhat off the beaten track and strangers to this part of the country.

'A cup o' tay, now?' replied roadman Joe. 'I make no doubt but Mrs Humble will make yer a cup o' tay at the shop.' And he jerked his thumb in the direction of that establishment.

'Oh, does she provide teas, without our having to journey up Magna?' asked the stranger with a sigh of relief.

'Not as a reg'lar do, she don't,' replied Joe, 'but Mrs Humble is one o' the obliging sort and weant begrudge yer a cup o' tay.'

'But, my good fellow,' expostulated the stranger, 'it would be an impertinence to ask the good lady to provide tea at a moment's notice unless she keeps a café.'

Joe placed his brush in the barrow, gave the man a pained look and remarked: 'You come along o' me, mister.'

He thrust open the shop door and called out, 'Are yer there, Mrs Humble?' at which a woman appeared through a doorway beyond the counter and inquired: 'What is it Joe—tobacco?'

'Nothing for missel, Mrs Humble,' replied Joe; 'there's a party here wants a cup o' tay. Can yer do owt for 'em?'

'Why, certainly if they don't mind waiting while I put the kettle on. Come inside, mister, come inside,' on seeing her two visitors hesitating in the doorway.

She conducted her visitors into her best parlour beyond the shop, apologizing for having nothing very special to lay before them. 'Just home-cured ham, fresh-laid eggs and home-made preserves.' They replied that these trifles would serve very nicely, and that what they wished for most was a cup of tea and a retreat from the hot sun in her cool and shaded parlour.

The kettle was soon put on to boil, and while they waited the visitors appraised the furnishings of the room. The furniture was of a bygone age, high-backed chairs upholstered in scrubby horsehair, with one side of the room taken up by a formidable dresser on which reposed several ornaments, books and a stuffed squirrel in a glass case. A grandfather clock ticked dolorously in one corner of the room with a little arc like a moustache cut in the dial which told the days of the week. The long diamond-paned window looked out on the street and had a window seat that formed an alcove in the wall.

Mrs Humble kept up a running commentary while she laid the table. She was one of those delightful persons who can wheedle information out of anyone, without seeming in the least to be a nosy Parker. A chatty person with bright, bird-like eyes who is also sharp-spoken may sound rather intimidating to a stranger, even though she is in reality a very amiable old soul.

'And have you travelled far this afternoon?' she inquired as she brewed the tea, and with similar guileless and friendly questions learned how on the day previous her visitors had journeyed from Chesterfield to Doncaster to attend a funeral, and how, to avoid the dusty turnpike this afternoon, they had explored the less frequented by-roads until they lost their whereabouts in this charming little village, and would be pleased if Mrs Humble could direct them as to the best route for Chesterfield.

'Why,' said Mrs Humble, 'I ain't never been as far away from home as that myself, but I would advise yer to go straight on through Magna till you come to Kingsmill and then ask again. But you should have asked Joe, him as brought you here—Joe knows his way about if anybody does. Aye,' she went on reflectively, 'I've known Joe Wrigley for years, longer than anyone else in this village; aye, we were a bit sweet on each other at one time, me and Joe, but owing to a bit of misfortune on Joe nothing came of it, and Joe's a man o' few words, and there's things he doesn't care to talk about.'

Such was the introduction of the stranger into our village. He was not exactly welcomed, for the village folk are suspicious of strangers, and it requires several years of permanent residence before an outsider can be admitted as an insider; but the process came about through the stranger, Mr Smith, a business man from town, along with his wife, falling in love with our pretty little village, and making subsequent trips to take tea at Mrs Humble's. Eventually, with helpful negotiations by Mrs Humble, the Smiths were able to secure apartments with George Western at Wheatlands Farm. They were becoming slightly better known

and might be said to have got a foot in the village. It was during
their third summer's stay at Wheatlands that a great decision was
made. They were enjoying afternoon tea in the farmer's garden
when George arrived home from the fields. He stayed a moment,
as he usually did, to ask where their rambles had led them during
the afternoon. The farmstead stood some way back from the
street on elevated ground, overlooking a couple of derelict
cottages, and perhaps for the want of something to make conversation Frank Smith remarked: 'Those cottages stand very
pleasantly down there—it's a pity they should have been allowed
to go to ruin.'

George smiled at his simplicity and replied: 'Nobody wants to
live in 'em, so there's not much sense in going into the expense
of repairing 'em.'

'That's strange,' replied Frank. 'Is there any reason apart from
their neglected condition why no one will live in them?'

'Young folk prefer Magna. There's nothing for young folk in
Parva—the place is dead,' replied George gloomily.

'That's a pity, for they stand very pleasantly just there. Who
owns them?'

'I own one of 'em,' conceded George, 'the one at the end of
the croft. Grandfather built it as a service cottage but, bless yer
life, a man will cycle back and forrard to Magna every day now
rather than be tied to the farm doorstep.'

'So there is nothing you can do with the place? You could not
sell it, I suppose?'

'Sell it? Nobody would buy property in this god-forsaken
place. I'd snatch anybody's hand off who offered me a hundred
pounds for it.'

'But surely it's worth more than a hundred pounds?' queried
Frank. He looked across at the derelict cottage, and presently
remarked: 'If you are in earnest, George, about the price I
should like to take a closer look at the place—that is after you
have had your tea of course.'

'Tea be blowed, mister!' burst out Farmer George. 'Let me
take yer across while yer in the humour.'

'There's some tea in the pot, Mr Western,' broke in Mrs Smith. 'It's quite fresh if you'd care to have it with us.'

George accepted a cup of tea and a cake, which he consumed standing, casting his eye towards the cottage the while as though fearful of its final collapse before he could negotiate a sale. The cottage needed a lot of repair. Several red tiles had slipped their mooring on the roof and besprinkled the ground; not a pane of glass was whole in any of the windows, and some of the frames were rotted and would need replacing. But the structure, the shell of the building, was sound, being built of dressed stone. A rotting porch surrounded the doorway, the larch posts of which were prevented from falling by the tenacious branches of a climbing clematis. Some three hundred square yards of garden covered with twitch-grass, docks and dandelion completed the property.

After showing his clients over the premises Farmer George remarked: 'Well, I'll leave yer to talk it over between yersels. I'm not trying to force a sale and, if yer decide agin it, it'll be all the same to me.' He walked away with a hopeful grin on his face.

Left to themselves Frank Smith and his wife made their decision and became the owners of Clematis Cottage (Mrs Smith's name for the property), and as soon as the property repairers had moved out they moved in, and spent most of their first summer painting and paper-hanging.

The cottage had two rooms downstairs and three bedrooms. At the gable end of the cottage was a lean-to coal- and wash-house combined, and after some search in the wilderness they discovered a lavatory modestly hiding itself behind a row of currant bushes at the end of the garden path.

CHAPTER TWO

Friends and Neighbours

ONE of the most gratifying results of living in the country is making friends with the neighbours. That is not to say that this happy state of affairs cannot exist in town, but that it does not thrive in a smoky atmosphere and fails to ripen if deprived of sunshine—one has only to watch the townsmen being carried up escalators like potatoes on the grid of a sorting-machine, rubbing unknown shoulders until they are poured off, good, bad or indifferent, to scurry away in haste with no recognition of the shoulder they had rubbed against. In the country to travel twice alongside a fellow countryman is to earn a nodding acquaintance, while a third meeting will make you 'friends and neighbours'. The villager is not so inarticulate as many townsmen consider him to be. His vocabulary may be limited to a few plain words, but it is to his credit that he expresses his views in crisp, plain language, putting as much in one sentence as would take up a whole paragraph by his more erudite cousins in town.

What a diversity of types is to be found even in so small a population as Parva. There is Harry Wilde the cowman, a man of most mild disposition, who cycles to work every morning from Magna to start milking at six o'clock prompt. He and Ralph the horse lad are the main members of the farm staff, good workmen but of no exciting interest. A more interesting personality is Billy Brunt who lives in one of the cottages, an erratic, non-dependable sort of fellow with an aversion from regular employment and subject to periodical outbursts of extreme thirst. Nevertheless Billy is a good workman when in the mood for a spell of honest toil, but he insists on piece rates, whether hedging, hoeing or cutting turnips. Having accomplished the work in about half the time his employer might have reasonably expected, Billy will go on the beer until his hard-earned money is exhausted.

The cottage folk were without exception weighed down by poverty, and yet were imbued with the spirit of helpfulness. The Smiths found this embarrassingly so at times. They would be busily cleaning down or decorating their rooms when a tap would come at the door and a woman's voice would inquire: 'Are you in, missis?' The caller would then step inside, profusely apologizing and offer her help, material or muscular, knowing how busy they must be then. She would comment on the pattern of the wallpaper and offer gratuitous advice on spring cleaning in general. She would stay chatting for a few minutes, then depart with renewed offers of help and a promise to call again. So through the day would come a steady flow of 'Can I help you's?', considerably holding up the work on hand. But not for worlds would the Smiths snub such friendly neighbours, though whether they came to help or to gossip and pry they were never certain.

One morning they had relaxed for coffee when their ears were assailed with a rhythmic 'swish-swish' from the direction of their garden. Looking out they were surprised to find a neighbour, Tom Pippin, in the garden, swinging a scythe. By this time half the garden was already laid out in neat winrows of twitch-grass, docks and dandelion.

'Sho's getten a bit out of hand, mister,' called out Tom, referring to the weeds.

'Yes, indeed,' was the reply, 'and thank you for coming along.' Mrs Smith coming to the door joined in with the remark: 'Would you care for a drink of coffee, mister? We are just having some ourselves.'

'That I would, missis, thank you—it's tough going through this.' Tom was invited indoors, and while he drank his coffee informed his hearers that he was a stonemason by trade, though owing to the decline in the stonemason's craft he was now the official lime-burner at Jonathan Keppel's quarries. He was on short time, he said, and thought he might earn a bob by straightening up the mister's garden. Which story so impressed the 'mister', Frank Smith, that he gave him a bob straight away and engaged him to put in a couple of hours each week at the same rate of remuneration. He was a man in his early sixties, grey-bearded, with those parts of his features that were visible above his beard tanned and wrinkled like a walnut-shell. He was pleased to accept the offer and, being a keen gardener himself, eventually converted Frank's wilderness into a garden of enchantment.

Another instance of good neighbourliness occurred one morning as the Smiths sat at breakfast. Farmer Western's horse lad called at the door, asking: 'Where do yer want this muck tipping, mister?'

Going to the door Frank Smith replied: 'I haven't ordered any manure. Are you sure you have come to the right place?'

'Sure,' replied the lad. 'Boss said Mr Smith!'

Frank Smith, having no enthusiasm for muck-spreading, maintained a stolid silence.

'Where will you have it, mister?' repeated the youth.

Being thus forced into action Frank gazed distastefully at the load of manure. 'Why, I hardly know,' he replied. 'Where would you advise?'

'Anentpetty,' advised the youth, all in one word, and began slinging the manure over the hedge to form a heap near the lavatory, or 'alongside the petty'.

In his early years at Nettleworth Parva Frank Smith was treated with amused contempt, as a figure of fun. They spoke to him with their tongues in their cheeks and grinned behind his back. They passed facetious remarks about his waxed mustachios and mimicked his precise and somewhat affected manner of speech, yet all the while showing great friendliness to his face on account of the pipes of tobacco he so generously dispensed. But George Western always held him in great respect, as was due to a man who had relieved him of a heap of rubble and given him a hundred pounds, and a firm friendship sprang up between the two houses, the farmhouse and the cottage, and many pleasant evenings were spent in each other's company.

George Western was a hefty, well-built fellow of medium height, fair-haired inclined to ginger and clean-shaven except for side whiskers. His wife too was robust and well proportioned. Their family consisted of two little girls, and also living in the farmhouse were Ada the servant-girl and Ralph the plough lad. Ralph was hired by the year, and had first come to Wheatlands on leaving school at fourteen years of age for the munificent sum of six pounds a year, with a two-pound rise for each succeeding year. He was now looked upon as one of the family. Farmer Western's nose was a brilliant red owing to his habit of taking large pinches of snuff, and another deplorable habit of his was chewing tobacco during the day time—he never smoked until the evening, nor would he allow anyone to smoke about the farm buildings. He farmed the largest acreage in the village, and was held in high regard both as farmer and neighbour.

There came a spell of hot, lovely weather towards the end of May, and one Monday morning Mrs Smith, like a good housewife, decided to do the washing. Her husband's part in this undertaking was merely to carry water from the village pump, on which they depended for their supply for all purposes. On this particular morning the old pump had a queer look about it. Its wooden arm, which normally hangs down when not in use, stood outstretched in a defiant attitude and Frank, having hung a bucket on the spout, gripped the arm and pulled it downward. It immediately sprang up again, almost taking Frank's chin along with it. He tried again, more cautiously, but with no better result than a gurgling sound out of the depths of the pump's bowels. A woman came to the door of a nearby cottage and called out: 'Sho wants priming, measter.'

'Priming?'

'Aye, owd yer bat.' And she went indoors.

She returned almost immediately carrying a pail of water. In a business-like manner she took the lid off the pump and gently poured the water inside, while vigorously jerking on the pump handle with her other hand. There were internal coughings and retchings as though the old pump was inclined to be sick, and after a few spasmodic gurglings it brought up a steady flow of water. Frank Smith filled his buckets, and hurried home thanking his stars for giving him such obliging neighbours. He slightly modified his views when close on his heels came the good neighbour with two more buckets of water, and at her heels a tiny tot of a girl carrying a half-gallon milk can, much too heavy for her tender years. Mrs Stubbs knew it was very probable that Mrs Smith would give her little girl a penny whether she lugged a great can of water or no, but to make it appear like earned income she had to bring a quart of pump water along. The woman stayed half an hour to chat, thus holding up the wash, then pleaded that she might stay and assist with the Smiths' laundry—she had in fact come with this fixed intention. Mrs Smith resolutely rejected the proposal, but Mrs Stubbs was persistent, and pleaded that Joe never earned more than fifteen shillings a week, and that he seldom put in a full week on account of his back. Thereupon Mrs Smith gave the woman a bottle of embrocation, advising her to rub it well into Joe's back. Mrs Stubbs was less hopeful of her husband's back being cured, and felt that an extra shilling or so at the wash-tub would ease her financial problems more effectively than any amount of rubbing of Joe's back, and cited Mrs Keppel at The Cedars as a satisfied customer, who would allow no one else to touch her linen save only the reliable Mrs Stubbs. Mrs Smith gave in, and engaged the good woman at one and sixpence the day with two meals, plus a bonus of a meaty bone to take home for Joe.

The Keppel family were among our friends and neighbours, though Mrs Keppel could hardly be called a friendly sort of person. Jonathan Keppel, the owner of several quarries in the district, was very reserved and a man of few words, but otherwise an agreeable gentleman. They lived at The Cedars, a large, brick-built house, the only brick residence in a village built entirely of stone. It was said that Mrs Keppel gave herself airs, which may have been true, for she never mixed with the village folk, nor even called at the little shop. They had two children, a girl named Julia and a young boy, rather delicate in his infant days, named Valentine. These two little dears were never seen playing with the vulgar village children, and attended a private school in Magna lest they became infected by rubbing shoulders with our native stock. The household included a nursery governess named Turbafield, who, after the children started attending grammar school, stayed on as lady companion to the mistress. Doubtless she bore a Christian name, too, but it was never used, Turbafield being considered sufficient for all occasions. One has to draw the line somewhere, and Miss Turbafield being an attractive young lady, educated and of pleasing manner, might have been mistaken for her betters, so that her mistress kept her in her place by drawing the line with a firm hand, and graciously rewarding her with thirty pounds per annum and her board.

On a much lower social scale was Bessie, the maid of all work. Whereas Turbafield took her meals along with the family, Bessie was confined to the culinary quarters to dine in solitude. Had Turbafield been free to choose her table she would no doubt have preferred the maid's company to the mistress's. The maid had one advantage over the governess in that she was referred to as Bessie instead of by her surname of Meeke. Her parents lived in the village, and Bessie had been engaged at half a crown per week, to be paid monthly. This caused some distress to Bessie, who expected payment every fourth week and seldom found it to work out so. Sometimes five weeks elapsed and Bessie, fearful yet desperate, would beg of Miss Turbafield to 'remind the missis'. Turbafield, ever obliging yet fearful herself, would approach the mistress on this delicate matter, when would ensue a terrific row, after which the mistress would come sweeping into the kitchen, declaring she did not know what servant-girls were coming to these days and, placing a half-sovereign on the mantelshelf out of Bessie's reach (for she was but a short young lady), would bounce out again with imprecations on big money and little work. It grieved Bessie much that she should draw the gentle Miss Turbafield into her troubles, whom she knew to have difficulties of her own from the same quarter, and only the loss of a week's pay prompted her to that extreme measure.

On six mornings of the week Bessie rose at five-thirty to cook and serve the master's breakfast, before he set off in the horse and trap at six-thirty for the stone quarries. She then prepared the family breakfast, which Miss Turbafield carried into the breakfast room, so that Bessie could set about scrubbing the wide expanse of tiled floor, blue and red, in her scullery. Then she had her own hurried breakfast before starting the day's work. She was of a bright and cheerful disposition, and looked forward with a thankful heart to the highlights of her situation such as staying in bed until seven-thirty on Sunday morning, having two hours off each week, usually after tea, and a half-day once per month, which, like her pay day, came erratically.

Another member of The Cedars, though scarcely of the household, was Johnny Jubb, the groom and gardener, usually referred to as Jubby, whose abode was the saddle-room where he was always on duty when the occasion required it. Jubby had no complaints to make about his situation; he was quite happy with his lot, and was indeed the envy of less happy men. The saddle-room where he dined and fed had a perpetual fire burning for the purpose of preserving the harness, and in the centre of the room was a small oblong table where Jubby took his meals. Except for a strong smell of leather, metal and harness polish, the atmosphere was snug and homely. Jubby had several perquisites which went with his situation, to wit a long green brass-buttoned overcoat, and a tall hard hat for when he required to drive the carriage, a hard bowler hat, yellow cord breeches and box cloth gaiters for when he was out with the master or conducting the children on their ponies. Along with these blessings each week he drew seven and sixpence, which he kept in a tin box in his bedchamber. This was a loft situated immediately over the saddle-room and reached by a broad stepladder, so that Jubby had always the benefit of the fire below stairs. A single bed, a dressing-table (to use a polite term) on which Jubby slung his collar and tie when he disrobed and a tin trunk completed the furnishing of Jubby's bedroom. Jubby was quite satisfied with his master, who treated him well, and was neither arrogant nor overbearing to his manservant. He even allowed him to walk down the village or up to Magna of an evening on asking leave of absence.

His feelings towards the mistress were less cordial. In his office as gardener he had to call at the house door with vegetables each morning where he was met by Bessie the maid, who relieved him of his offerings, for though Jubby had been there for several years, never once had he been allowed over the doorstep. Such was Jubby, the general factotum at The Cedars, eternally chewing tobacco and scattering the juice abroad in defiance of decency or good taste, to the annoyance of his mistress and with an utter disregard of the principles of hygiene.

CHAPTER THREE

In Quires and Places Where They Sing

CHURCH life in Nettleworth Parva was sharply divided between the Anglican and the Nonconformist persuasion, though neither church nor chapel was of any architectural merit. The most noticeable feature was the estrangement that existed between these two worthy bodies. The Anglican church, a mere hut built of corrugated iron, was an offshoot of the parent church of St Giles in Nettleworth Magna. The Nonconformist place of worship belonging to the Wesleyans was a wooden construction. The elect, that is to say the 'best' people of the village, attended the church services, they being respectable folk with a sense of reverence and orderliness in their worship and sticklers for ritual and observances. The Wesleyans, however, were more virile in their worship; they believed in a boisterous brotherhood and sang Moody and Sankey choruses at the tops of their voices, to the shocked dismay of the Anglicans, who saw in this a lack of reverence towards the Almighty. The Nonconformists too had a flair for Revivalist meetings, and indulging in the songs of Torrey-Alexander missions. With this state of animosity between two sects it is highly improbable that there will ever be unity among the children of God.

Distinguished among the Church worshippers is Jonathan Keppel. Dignified of mien, and carrying his tall silk hat in which repose his kid gloves, he walks up the aisle accompanied by his wife, who is arrayed in silks and wears a large straw hat bedecked with flowers. They are followed by their two children and Miss Turbafield, who always enters the pew first along with her little charges. Having become seated they all bow their heads on the pew in front and, so say their detractors, count fifty before sitting upright. The only other person worthy of special notice is Miss Lovibond, the schoolmistress, a rather dowdy-looking creature wearing a black hat trimmed with red roses. What is noteworthy about Miss Lovibond is that she always bows to the altar and sits in utter loneliness in the very front pew, for which act of piety she has earned the scorn of Mistress Keppel. The main pillars of the Chapel are the Robinson family and Mrs Humble from the shop. Edward Robinson is a farmer with a close-cropped beard, and on Sundays he wears the inevitable tall silk hat. Besides being a fairly successful farmer, he finds time to attend to the steward-ship of the chapel, along with the office of Sunday school super-intendent. His eldest daughter, Miss Harriet, is the organist, as well as taking a class at Sunday school. Strangely enough, though the Robinsons and Mrs Humble are the only people of note at the chapel, it equals the church in the size of its congregation, being greatly patronized by the lower orders on account of its singing.

There are a few who attend no place of worship, but their number is very small, for Parva offers no other attraction on a Sabbath evening, and Christmas and other Church festivals, including harvest, finds both churches packed with worshippers, whether they be devout Christians or merely bored rustics.

The curate who takes the services at the Anglicans is the Rev. Gilbert Malham, a fair-haired young fellow in his late twenties. He cycles down from Magna each Sunday morning, conducts his service, then has to ride or push his cycle back again up the steep Magna hill. If there is to be an evening service the journey has to be repeated. Being a very likeable young man he was sometimes invited to lunch at The Cedars and sometimes to the Smiths' at Clematis Cottage. It was in this way that a firm friend-ship sprang up between Frank Smith and the young curate. He was a keen young fellow and showed great concern about the social and religious stupor that had settled on the village.

'Is there nothing we can do to get something going in the place?' he asked one afternoon as the two men sat resting after lunch in the Smiths' best parlour.

'Why, Gilbert, the same thought has struck me,' replied Frank, 'and last week I called on Miss Lovibond at the school to ask whether it would be permissible to hold a gramophone recital in her schoolroom. She is making inquiries of the school board.'

'School board, fiddlesticks!' replied the curate bluntly. 'This is the church school, so carry on, and I will be everlastingly grateful for your interest.'

The result of this Sunday afternoon's chat at Clematis Cottage was a series of recitals in the village schoolroom. The gramophone had recently become a popular means of entertainment among the middle class, and had quite replaced the old phonograph with its cylindrical records. Frank Smith owned machines of both varieties, though his wife, a skilled pianist, scorned both, saying that she could not abide tinned stuff whether it was meat or music. Nevertheless the gramophone evenings in the schoolroom became popular, and when Mrs Smith tauntingly asked, 'What about the old phonograph, Frank? What do you intend to do with that thing?' the reply was: 'I suggest you give it to Mrs Stubbs next washday.'

Mrs Stubbs accepted the machine with thanks, and the last to be heard of the transaction was that Joe had raffled it off in the Red Lion at Magna, then spent one week on the beer and two weeks in bed with a bad back.

The little schoolroom was packed with about twenty adults and every child in the village. A varied and comprehensive programme had been arranged which included the Hallelujah Chorus, excerpts from Beethoven concertos and pieces for both organ and violin by Bach. It was the opinion in some quarters that this music would be quite out of reach of most of the audience, but it proved otherwise, though they may have shown more acclaim for 'Sweet Rosie O'Grady' and that rollicking nonsense 'You've got a long way to go':

> Once on a donkey's back I tried
> Dick Turpin's ride to York.
> When suddenly the moke stood still
> And I got off to walk.

'Twas miles out in the country,
And he wouldn't move for me,
I asked the cop where London was,
'Lord love-a-duck,' said he,

'You've got a long way to go
You've got a long way to go.'
He gave the Jerusalem moke a smack,
And planted a pin in his Union Jack,
He wouldn't move for me,
The copper said, 'What-ho,
You'd better get hold of the donkey's rudder,
For you've got a long way to go.'

Everyone joined in the chorus and without doubt the most popular tunes with the cottage folk were folk-songs, and everyone went home happily singing some refrain or other after two solid hours of Edison Bell records.

As the crowd dispersed the school caretaker stepped forward and confided: 'Mr Smith, I want to apologize for our Joe; he says he would ha' liked to ha' come, but as he has no ear for music he's gone to spend an hour at the King's Head.'

In spite of lack of support from Joe Stubbs these gramophone concerts proved very popular. Furthermore they endeared Frank Smith to the village community, and the veiled amusement and caustic comment gave place to a genuine regard for the stranger who had settled among them. They accepted him as a neighbour, waxed 'tachios and all.

One day Frank Smith called in Mrs Humble's shop for some small purchase. Mrs Humble never hurried her customers. She loved to chat, though never maliciously, and a purchase which need take up no more than a minute she could extend to half an hour. So after expressing her views on the state of the weather, the prospects of hay and corn harvest, and the latest editions of births and deaths she remarked:

'I hear you have a very good piano at your house, Mr Smith?'

'Yes, a fairly good instrument, Mrs Humble.'

'Now isn't that nice? And do you play, Mr Smith, or is your wife the musician?'

'We both play occasionally, but only my wife can be called an accomplished musician.'

Then, as though changing the subject, Mrs Humble remarked: 'Harriet Robinson has taken an ulcerated sore throat.'

'Oh dear, how very distressing.'

'And she won't be able to play the organ on Sunday for the children's anniversary.'

'How very unfortunate, and can you find no one to deputize?'

'That's just it, sir, I was wondering when you came into the shop, and knowing as you have a piano, I says to myself, Praised be the Lord, here comes our organist.'

'But, my good woman,' expostulated Mr Smith, 'a piano is not an organ, quite a different instrument. I do assure you I scarcely know a thing about organ playing, otherwise I would be pleased to help you out.'

'Aye, Mr Smith, I'm sure you would,' went on Mrs Humble with calm unconcern, 'and the service starts at two-thirty—aye, it's a true saying, a friend in need is a friend indeed; and here's yer stuff—ninepence, if yer please. It's what they call an American organ, but you will know what that means, and here's the key to the chapel door in case you'd like to practise afore Sunday. And so saying the good lady thrust in his hand a monstrous key along with his groceries.

Frank Smith explained to his wife the awful predicament he was in to which his wife's retort was: 'Look here, Frank, seeing that we have the key, and that it is only for Sunday afternoon, shall we go and see what can be done? I used to play hymn tunes on the organ years ago, and to oblige the old lady I don't mind taking on the job just for once.'

They went that same afternoon, and after some practice Mrs Smith announced her willingness to oblige on anniversary Sunday. They found their first attendance at a children's anniversary most interesting. The children who, when one saw them playing in the street, were mostly unwashed little ragamuffins, were on this occasion trim and clean in their Sunday best. Looking at their happy faces, somewhat self-conscious because of their elevated position on the platform, one realized the virtue of clean linen and the close affinity between soap and salvation. They sang sweetly, both in unison and solo, and said their pieces with bashful heroism. One was struck with the transformation of Quiddy, the eldest son of the degenerate Billy Brunt, whom we first met driving home Farmer Western's milk cows. He was now appearing under his Sunday name of Willie Brunt, and wearing a decent though cheap-looking knickerbocker suit of a salt and pepper hue, along with a deep and starched collar, which he wore with evident discomfort.

The service was conducted by Farmer Edward Robinson, and alternated between the singing of hymns, saying of pieces and a scripture lesson from St Matthew's Gospel on the talents. There was a matter-of-factness about Farmer Robinson's mode of speech that would have shocked our curate with his sing-song intonations as smacking of impiety.

'And now we are to have a piece by Willie Brunt, entitled, "The New Leaf",' Farmer Robinson announces.

Gallant and undismayed Willie rose to his feet:

'*The New Leaf*

I mean to turn over a nice new leaf,
And never cause anyone pain nor grief,
And always use my handkerchief.
If anyone hits me, I'll be so meek,
And simply turn the other cheek.
Careful too on how I speak.
I will always speak in gentle tones,
At dear little birdies I will never throw stones,
Nor chase the cat that nobody owns.
When shall I begin? Why not now?
And so, kind friends, I make my bow,
Determined for ever to keep my vow.'

Willie sat down amid smiles of approval, and Edward Robinson, eyeing him sternly for a moment, remarked: 'I hope thou lives up to it, my boy.'

Several more pieces were said, of like improving quality, and several more solos, duets and choruses were sung. Then Mr Robinson came to his piece. He was a sincere and pious old fellow for all his uncultivated manner of speech, and after announcing his address as from the twenty-fifth chapter of St Matthew's Gospel, began:

'And now, childer, what think you to the man who was given only one talent? It wasn't fair to him. He was given a raw deal, eh, up agin those clever fellows who could turn their hand to a number of jobs. No wonder he was discouraged, and said "What's the use?" Aye, but that's the wrong meaning of it; this parable is about man's responsibility towards God and his fellow men. We've a responsibility towards God and also towards our fellow men, so every one of us is given a talent for doing certain work. So we have a talented musician, a talented artist, a talented artist craftsman. Some people are given only one talent, and some are given five; but the number of talents we possess don't matter, and the man with one talent is as important as the man with many talents. Take the pipes in a church organ, for instance: some large and some small, but all of different tones. Supposing now the smaller pipes said, "It's no use me trying to compete with those big fellows" and refused to take their part—why, childer, the whole organ would be out o' gear, and nothing but discord would issue instead of the perfect harmony which the Master required when He issued to us our respective talents. So do not lose heart, my dears, nor think it unfair that God has given more power to one person than to another. We are not to be rewarded for the number of talents we were given but for our way of using them.

'Our talents are increased by use, and unless we do use them, be they one talent or five, they will be taken from us. Practice makes perfect, and so we find the musician, the cricketer or the footballer can only maintain his talent or increase it by regular practice. If he gets swelled head and thinks he has no need to practise, then when he comes to perform he will find his talent has been taken away from him. So, childer, whatever talents you possess use them for all you are worth, work them hard, and they will increase in value and you will be made masters over many things.

'According to the parable these talents are not our own but were loaned to us by God to be used in His service—that is to say for the benefit of all mankind. Profit is only of secondary importance, and the musician's greatest motive is to give pleasure and happiness to all who care to listen. So with all artists, and so with cricketers and athletes who use their talents for the honour of the team and all for the glory of God.

'The reward? "Well done, good and faithful servant, I will make thee master over many cities." Only that fearful wretch who went and hid his talent is left out.'

CHAPTER FOUR

The Rustic Swain

ON THE Saturday morning following the children's anniversary service young Quiddy was indulging in the innocent sport of bird's-nesting. He had not forgotten, and had no intention of forgetting, his promise to turn over a new leaf, besides which, though he was no angel and did not in the least resemble an angel, he never wantonly destroyed birds' nests. What happened was just ill luck, which might come to any one of us. He had left the wood and was crossing the fallow on his way back to the village, when he came across a plover's egg laid on the fallow. He picked it up and examined it, a lovely yellowish-green egg with brown spots on the thicker end. He was about to replace it when he noticed Ralph, the horse lad, driving three horses abreast in the heavy harrows coming straight in a line with the plover's egg. It would certainly be destroyed by the horses' hoofs or the harrow teeth, so Quiddy, still filled with good intentions, placed the egg in his pocket and continued his way home.

On that same Saturday morning little Val Keppel was playing with his hoop along the flower-bordered parental drive. He was not allowed off the premises unless under the care of Miss Turbafield or the groom, but this morning the spirit of adventure must have possessed him, for he opened the ornamental iron gates and trundled his hoop on the roadway. He looked the picture of childish innocence as he tripped along wearing a white and blue striped sailor suit, with sailor hat to match on which was emblazoned in large letters, 'H.M.S. Valiant'. Unfortunately he had not travelled far when he met with young Quiddy, who paused to eye little Val over with disfavour.

Mindful of his recent conversion Quiddy decided to be friendly. 'Hallo, kid,' he greeted. 'Whatcher doing?'

'I am playing with my hoop,' replied Val primly.

'I thought as much,' said Quiddy, adding: 'Say, let's have a go!' At which Val stepped hastily backward and said, 'Shan't!'

'Gurn, I don't want to take it from yer. I say, Val, would yer like a bird's egg, a pewit, sithee?'

'No, thank you,' replied Val in disdain. 'Mama says it's naughty to take little birdies' eggs.'

'Yar . . . what a milksop yer are. Here, owd yer hand out.'

Too timid to refuse Val held out his hand, on which Quiddy, with a burst of laughter, crushed the contents of the plover's egg. With a yell of dismay Val wiped his egg-stained hand on his nice clean suit, then as though inspired by the name on his sailor hat kicked his tormentor on the shins. This was too much for Quiddy. It didn't come under the order of reformation, nor of turning the other cheek, and unmindful of his vows he struck little Val on the nose. There was a yell of pain and terror which brought Mama fluttering on to the scene, holding wide her flowing skirts after the manner of a motherly hen spreading its wings in protection of its young.

Quiddy had vanished so, after administering first aid to the wounded, Mrs Keppel hunted out her groom and gardener, Jubby, to arrest that loathsome boy and take him to the police. Jubby naturally inquired which boy it was, upon which his mistress called him an ass, and told him to find out quickly or it would be the worse for him. In Jubby's opinion it would be 'one o' Billy Brunt's lads', so on this slight clue Jubby called at Brunt's cottage. Billy Brunt senior is an easy-going individual, with little concern about what might come tomorrow. His wife follows much the same pattern of life, and a general untidiness prevails inside the house. The Brunts are a family of eight, of which Quiddy, aged eleven, is the eldest, and there is always a smell of baby clothes lying around waiting to be washed.

Jubby, looking in at the open doorway, discovered Mrs Brunt seated in the rocking-chair, singing to her youngest born which she bounced upon her knee to the soothing words:

'Dance a-doodie, diddie,
What shall thi Mammy do widdie?
Thou must sit on her lap,
And sho'l gie thee some pap.
Dance a-doodie diddie.'

The song and dance stopped abruptly on seeing a visitor at the door and the woman called out: 'Why, if it isn't Jubby! Come thi ways in, Mr Jubb.' Then turning to her eldest born: 'What for are yer skulking back there, Quiddy? Shift them mucky napkins off that chair so's mister can sit down.'

Jubby gave the pile of baby linen a disdainful glance, chewed hard on his plug and spat viciously out into the garden. 'No, thank yer, missis,' he said. 'I'm not sitting down. What I've come for is a word or two wi' that limb o' mischief.' Turning to that 'limb o' mischief' he growled: 'You, there! What yer been up to this morning?'

'Me, sir?' replied Quiddy with a look of innocent surprise; 'I've only been bird's-nesting in Highbrake Wood.'

'Thou'rt a lying young imp I make no doubt. Some'dys given our young gentleman a rare wallop on his noase, and Mrs Keppel has sent me to take him to the bobby, whoever he was. Now spake the truth, young man, has thou been near our place this morning?'

'I tell you, I've been in Highbrake Wood all morning.'

'Well, that's a corker!' said Jubby, addressing the woman. He planted one foot firmly on a certain spot on the kitchen floor, saying, 'Highbrake's here'—he firmly planted his other foot in another position—'and The Cedars is there. Now, it sounds to sense as your lad couldn't ha' been in Highbrake, and a hitting of our young gentleman down at our place at one and the same time, therefore I must regretfully say, it wern't him who done it.'

'It couldn't ha' been him, mister,' agreed the woman, adding: 'There's another reason why it couldn't ha' been him. I gives 'em all a brew o' hoarhound, else cammomile flowers, o' Sat'dy mornings to keep their bowels in order. Keeps 'em quiet, they don't leave home far while that's working, so I reckon our

Quiddy wouldn't exert himself this morning to wallop Master Val on the nose.'

'No, mebbe not, but he's a proper young limb is that lad o' yours,' ventured Jubby. 'Onyroad, I'd better tak' him along wi' me to see what the mistress thinks o' him.'

He turned to beckon the young culprit forward, but Quiddy had gone.

'Why, the lad's takken off!' exclaimed Jubby in surprise.

'Aye, he had senna this morning—it takes 'em quick,' said Mrs Brunt.

Jubby returned to The Cedars, wondering what excuse to make to the mistress for his failure, and Quiddy's mother continued her ditty of 'Dance a-doodie diddie'.

It was Saturday evening of the same day, a lovely warm evening towards the end of May, and all the world of Nettleworth Parva was resting from its week of strenuous toil. Nature is a great leveller, and the townsman cannot maintain a superior stance over the simple rustic when surrounded by rustic scenery. Mr and Mrs Smith in their garden at Clematis Cottage were enjoying the view over the hedge where Farmer Western's two brood mares were nursing their respective foals. George Western was very proud of his stable of horses, particularly of the two mares which presented him with two foals each year, and this year the grey mare Flower was rearing a lovely little foal of a sooty brown colour, almost black, while Jewel, the dark brown, had a definitely dark brown foal. It was a picture to charm, with a bunch of calves to give brighter colour to the scene.

Farmer Western walked across and stopped by the hedge to have a chat. In the course of their conversation Frank remarked:

'Isn't it odd that Flower, a white horse, should have a black foal?'

Farmer George smiled. 'It may seem odd to you, Frank, but I should think it odd if Flower gave birth to a white foal, for there was never yet a foal born that colour.'

'But what about Prince, the three-year-old dappled grey?' asked Frank doubtingly.

c

'Prince was as black as this youngster when he was born,' averred George,' so are all foals that eventually become grey. Black as soot the first year, then peppered with black and white during their second year. At three years old they become iron-grey, and from then up to seven years they become the beautiful dappled greys at their very best. After seven years the black dapples gradually disappear, so that at about ten years of age the horse becomes grey or white.'

'So you can tell a grey horse's age by its colour?'

'Well, not with any certainty. Some lose their dapples sooner than others, but if anyone tried to sell me a white horse as a seven year old I would query his statement.'

'You would look the gift horse in the mouth, eh, George?'

'That's very much guesswork after a young horse has got its four-year-old teeth,' replied George, 'though there are certain signs by which one can judge a horse's age. The front teeth grow long, especially in the case of a town horse, who eats all his food out of a manger and never has a chance to nibble with his front teeth, as does the farm horse at grass, who is fond of nibbling the young twigs on the hedgerow. When a horse is getting on in years deep hollows develop over his eyes, and these are a sure sign of decay in vigour whatever age he may be.'

Foals, calves, growing lambs and thriving chickens—such was the scene on all three farms this May evening, with special notice of Farmer Robinson's hunter mare, Vashti, suckling her fifth successive foal, and a notable winner in her class at all the local shows.

Where was Ralph the plough lad on this sunny evening? He had hurriedly got washed and changed after tea, brought out his bike and pedalled like fury up Magna hill to be in time to see the seventh instalment of *The Exploits of Elaine* showing at the Globe Picture Palace. So far he had not missed one instalment, and it would be a pity that he should, for this indulgence provided his one excitement from one Saturday evening to the next.

Sunday was always looked upon as a holy day by the village

folk. Not that they were deeply religious, but they respected the saying, 'A Sabbath well spent brings a week of content', and it was supposed that any gainful labour done on Sunday would be marred by the devil for the rest of the week.

Mr Jubb, alias Jubby the groom and gardener at The Cedars, had a great regard for Sunday afternoon, especially in summer when his horses were turned out to grass for the week-end in the nearby paddock. He then cast off his livery and arrayed himself in long trousers, buttoned boots, a hard hat and a decent black coat adorned with two large buttons in the small of the back. It had become a tradition with Jubby to take tea with a friend of his at Magna on alternate Sunday afternoons, and for his friend to repay the visit on the following Sunday and take tea with Jubby in his little bothy. How it all started no one seemed to know, but there it was, and on Jubby's Sunday at home Bessie the maid always brought out a double ration of tea in anticipation of Jubby's guest.

Jubby's friend was in the same 'line' as Jubby, a gentleman's groom and gardener; his name—Walter. He worked for John Brookfield, Esq., the last of an ancient family who had formerly owned the large estate of the two Nettleworths. Riotous living, which usually includes slow horses and fast women, had so reduced the revenues of the estate that when young John came into possession he sold the ancestral hall and took up his abode at The Spital. He was a strange, much talked of old fellow these days, usually referred to as 'owd Johnny'. He never married, but lived in seclusion in that solitary farmhouse, a well-bred gentleman in the true sense of the word, a bookworm and a recluse. The community was filled with amused contempt for Johnny's attempt to keep up the appearance of past grandeur by dining off silver plate, though according to report the fare consisted of nothing more than biscuits and cheese. Strangely enough some half-dozen of the old staff remained faithful to him, and refused to be dismissed until infirmity or death cancelled their engagement. So at this present time the permanent staff had been reduced to an old housekeeper, almost blind, and old Walter, who acted as coachman for the one-horse carriage, both of them as timeworn and debilitated as their owner.

There was nothing of particular interest in either Jubby or his friend Walter to attract them to each other. They were just good friends who met once a week to exchange views, and to comment on their respective gardens and their horses. Sometimes they would sit the whole evening without exchanging a word, then when it was time to depart old Walter would be most profuse with his thanks for a lively, well-spent evening.

There was the occasion, too, when Jubby remarked: 'I've bought a pair o' new boots this week; them owd ons were crippling me.'

'Aye, it's grievous to be wearing ill-fitting boots,' replied Walter, drawing his feet under his chair so as to hide their bursting seams.

'A pair o' good boots too,' went on Jubby; 'it ed be a pity to throw 'em away. I wonder, now, Walter, would you do me a favour?'

'Why o' course, lad, if it's anyways possible,' was the reply.

'I reckon you takes the same size as me in boots, so if you'd try these for a week or two just to pad 'em down I might wear 'em agen myself some time.'

In such artless chicanery did Jubby help his old friend, with an occasional old coat or partly worn linen, for the Keppels were particular about their groom looking spick and span.

The village folk were individualists. They grew true to type, and one knew what to expect of each individual. Even Joe Stubbs never varied. But the farm men were the most worthy of notice. That they loved their work was very evident, but why they should do so was less evident, seeing that they worked longer hours for less pay than did the quarrymen, who finished work at one o'clock on Saturday noon. George Western's man, Ralph, and Edward Robinson's man, Charlie Butcher, were typical examples, for having put in six long days at the plough they must needs take a walk across the fields on Sunday morning to see if their ploughs were still there. Or so it would seem, though a friendly rivalry existed between Ralph and Charlie as to who could turn the neatest furrow or draw the straightest ridge in the turnip and potato rows.

One reprehensible blot had Charlie Butcher; he always carried a catapult around with him on these Sunday morning walks, whereas Ralph was satisfied to live and let live. Charlie's ammunition consisted of small pebbles, which lay in plenty on the drive encircling the frontage to the farmhouse. Although, on his master catching him in the act, he had been forbidden to denude the drive of any more pebbles, Charlie still continued his morning stroll with his coat pocket sagging with the weight of the stones. His target was anything that moved, with a preference for rabbits. His toll of kills was never very great, for a catapult is not the most effective of weapons on a running target. Charlie, who was married, lived in the farm cottage rent free on seventeen shillings per week in cash, along with a quart of milk each day and two sacks of potatoes each year. Taken all in all, with his cash and perquisites, Charlie was not in desperate need of a freshly killed rabbit for his table; but some bloodthirsty streak in his nature prompted him to slaughter anything that moved, even to a solitary crow flying overhead.

Having critically examined the ploughlands, and maybe the woods, they invariably ended their peregrinations in the horse pasture, at any rate in the summer months when their horses were out at grass. The shire horse was their god, whether they worshipped other gods or not; they bowed down before him and made obeisance. Even the dog, from time immemorial the boon companion of man, never exacted as high a degree of homage and reverence as did the horse, be it shire, hunter or trapper. The dog is a shapeless animal and wins our affection by fawning upon our notice, whereas the horse draws our affection and regard by his noble bearing and beauty of outline, his shapely proportions of proudly arched neck and deep chest, and the gentle curve of his back and rump. Moreover the horse never fawns nor begs a favour, but accepts our offering of a sugar lump or a crust of bread as his royal right. He never cries out nor makes a murmur in pain or fear; the only time a horse gives voice is in a whinny of recognition or a neigh of pleasure. In times of stress, pain or fear he clenches his teeth and remains mute; a groan escapes him only when his agony gets too much for him, showing that with all his dignity and lordly bearing he is but mortal.

It's strange how much the rustics love their horses. One would be inclined to think that after six long days in their company the men would be glad to lose sight of them on the Sabbath. This deep affection is not bestowed on other animals, the cow, for instance. Admittedly a calf is a lovesome creature, but when its horns increase in stature its comeliness decreases in proportion. In form and in movement the cow has nothing to win our affection. It is a short-sighted beast, making ungainly progress with its head not far from the ground, sniffing its way along with its ears shading its eyes, the better to see any object in its path.

Sheep are the dirtiest of all farm animals—they just cannot help it. All other animals have some method of doing their toilet; some lick themselves or lick each other; some scratch, rub or roll; all are insistent on bodily cleanliness. Excepting only the sheep. With a thick fleece of wool wrapped round its body what can the poor creature do? It can neither scratch nor rub to any effect; consequently its fleece becomes filthy and verminous, so much so that the law decrees that sheep must be annually dipped in a strong solution of disinfectant to counteract this oversight of Nature.

There is no animal so clean and respectable as the pig, albeit he has been grossly libelled with a reputation for filth. True he loves to wallow in the mire for an hour, but this he uses as Fuller's soap to loosen the 'bartles of his skin', and afterwards will spend an infinity of time rubbing his deep sides against a stone or brick wall, until his skin shines with perfect cleanliness. Given plenty of straw no animal is so particular as the pig in keeping his bed clean and dry, and it is the fault of man if the pig fouls the corner wherein he makes his bed. It may be thanks to Piggy's regard for hygiene that he is troubled with fewer diseases of the flesh than any other animal, and he deserves our commendation rather than our scorn.

Like the rustic swains the three farmers in the village might be termed individualists, in that each one specialized in his own type of farming. They were all as one in that their farms were what are termed 'mixed farms', mostly corn growing, with a small herd of dairy cattle from which the farmer's wife derived her 'pin-money' from the sale of butter and cheese. The Robinsons specialized in poultry on a large scale. In the spring and early summer the orchard was filled with coops, chicks, ducks and turkeys. It was a busy undertaking, and the young sons of Charlie Butcher were conscripted into service as each child reached the age of discretion and ability to dole out the chick food and water to the long line of coops. It is strange to recall how those three boys of Charlie Butcher's revelled in helping Miss Harriet with her chicks, and fairly fell over one another as to who should get there first and who should serve the greatest number of coops—and yet on leaving school not one of them kept to the farm. They had had enough even at that tender age, and decided on industrial labour with Saturday afternoon off.

There was no such bustling activity at George Western's farm. His chick rearing was on a moderate scale and well under the management of his wife and family, with occasional help from Quiddy, whose visits were more noticeably frequent when the apples were ripe in the orchard.

The other farm, situated on the edge of the village, was tenanted by Richard Crookes and was only fifty acres in extent. His speciality was pigs, and their subsequent attendants—rats. He likewise kept geese and guinea-fowl, both of which created much clamour in an otherwise lonely place. He was a miserly, crotchety old fellow, usually referred to as 'Dicky Drybones', and had a half-witted youth working for him for the simple reason that no one with his full wits would put up with the old curmudgeon.

CHAPTER FIVE

Otherworthies

THOUGH there were a few of the older generation who could neither read nor write, illiteracy was not widespread, and even Billy Brunt could spell out his name sufficiently well to be decipherable. The most remarkable thing was the number of books each family possessed. There was not a cottage in the village but had a row of books on the dresser, well-bound books in embossed covers, many of them wearing the tissue-paper in which they left the shop. Though these were mostly school prizes, they were held in great reverence by the parents, and no one was allowed to open a book with unwashed hands. Perhaps they carried their regard for books to the extreme, but it was a fact that the less able they were to read a book themselves the greater was their desire to know of its contents. Thus it was that the 'good reader' child read aloud to the family, not once but often, and it would be useless to tell them that these stories were fiction. To them Tom and Maggie Tulliver became real flesh and blood people, and so were Silas Marner and Harriet Beecher Stowe's Uncle Tom.

It is not always true to say 'like father like son'. Ben Travis's brood were all bright children who had passed as 'excellent' in most subjects at school, whereas Ben himself was rather a dull sort of fellow. Esther, the eldest born, had carried home many book prizes, and the Travis family even possessed a bookcase in which to keep them, which placed them on a slightly higher social scale than those who kept their books on the dresser.

Ben Travis was a coal-dealer in a very small way among a community who preferred wood fires which they obtained free from the nearby woods. The summer price of coal was twelve shillings per ton, which in winter rose to fourteen shillings. The farmers, or anyone who owned a horse and cart, bought their coal direct from the pit head, while the labouring folk who could seldom afford the vast price of a ton of coal, were supplied by Ben with hundredweights, varying in price from tenpence to one shilling. This job, along with three acres of land on which Ben grew oats for his horses and potatoes for his household, lifted Ben above the level of a labouring man without greatly enhancing his financial position. He had the sorriest pair of nags imaginable, neither of which appeared to be capable of shafting a ton of coal down Magna hill, and it was not uncommon to find one of the poor creatures lying down at the foot of the hill with the load of coal on his back.

One such incident occurred when Frank Smith, having been advised by Mrs Humble, who always bought her stock of coal at summer price, called on Ben to supply him with two tons to be delivered at Ben's convenience. The first ton travelled safely down the hill, and arrived without mishap at Clematis Cottage. A gawky sort of youth was in charge, and he halted the horse at the entrance to Frank's yard which rises rather steeply off the roadway.

'Gup, Jasper,' he said presently in encouragement.

Jasper looked at that short, steep rise and shook his head.

'Gup, Jasper,' said the youth in a sterner voice, accompanied by a tap from the switcher he carried.

Jasper tightened his chains, then quietly lay himself down with the load of coal on top of him. He seemed quite content with his situation, and neither the youth nor Smith appeared to know what to do to improve things. Fortunately the roadman, Joe Wrigley, arrived on the scene and took command.

'Sit on his yed, thou fooil, sit on his yed!' he shouted to the perplexed youth. It was then noticed that the animal was threshing its head on the ground as though bent on suicide, so the youth gingerly sat on its head, upon which the horse ceased to exert itself further. A crowd of two women and one man had now gathered to view the accident, upon which Joe addressed the man with, 'Here's a nice how d' yer do, Tushy lad—t'owd hoss has gone down. Gie 'us a hand will'ta to undo his chains.'

So with the youth sitting on the horse's head as a sort of sedative, the two men loosened the chains and, aided by the onlookers, the cart was pushed backwards off the horse's limbs, and the wretched animal induced to rise to its feet. The coal was tipped on the roadway and the horse was sent home with the empty cart along with much gratuitous advice to the carter on the methods of horse keeping. The crowd dispersed and Joe, before returning to his road sweeping, said confidingly: 'Allus sit on its yed, mister, when a hoss gets down—allus sit on its yed.'

Left alone to face a load of coal tipped on the roadway instead of by his coal-house door Frank Smith took two small buckets and a fire shovel to commence operations. He had barely made a start when Joe the roadman reappeared with his wheelbarrow and a large shovel. Frank raised objections, saying he could manage without help, and how Joe would be in trouble if the council found out he was wheeling in someone's coal when he should be cleaning the roadway.

'And ain't I clearing the roadway now, mister?' replied Joe. 'How can I sweep along here wi' all this coal scattered about?'

Such logic was unanswerable, so Joe was allowed to continue his good work, and was rewarded with a cup of cocoa and a shilling. The second load of coal arrived without mishap, and all future stocks of winter fuel were carted by his friend George Western, free of charge, which was good for the Smiths but bad for the business of Ben Travis.

Another otherworthy character was the man whom Joe had addressed as Tushy. His baptismal name had been Samuel, but his upper teeth as he grew up protruded under his upper lip in such a ludicrous manner that he became more popularly known as Tushy. His wife being always addressed as Mrs Whysall it may be assumed that Tushy had a lawful right to be addressed as Mr Samuel Whysall. But it's useless trying to flout popular choice, and as 'Tushy' he was known to all and sundry, even when age and decay deprived him of his teeth.

Tushy was a man of many parts, rat-catcher, rabbit-catcher

and chimney-sweep, though he did little business in the last-named capacity, since most of the Parva-ites cleared their own chimneys of soot by firing an armful of straw therein. His method of catching rats or rabbits was with ferrets, of which Tushy kept about half a dozen in a box in his garden shed, and these he tended with loving care, which could be nauseating to watch by anyone with no affection for the bloodthirsty little creatures. When ferreting he carried the little wretches in a sack half filled with hay or, if the day were very cold, he would carry a ferret inside his shirt to warm itself on his bare chest. He played with and fondled them as some would a kitten or a puppy, and, blood-thirsty creatures as they are, they never bit the hand that fed them. They were indeed evil-looking creatures with lithe, sinuous bodies that wreathed to and fro on their bed of hay, with their nozzles and wicked pink eyes turned upward in search of food, for it is an axiom that a working ferret must be kept warm and hungry. Another striking feature about Tushy was that he could capture his rats alive, without the aid of ferrets, traps or any other artifice. It may seem unbelievable, but he could call them out of their holes by simply making a sucking sound with his mouth, as effectively as did the Pied Piper with his pipe. He practised this method effectively one day at Common End Farm. Tushy had a regular practice in keeping the rats down for old Drybones, making at least two visits during the course of each year. Dicky Drybones was pleased to get rid of his rats, but it hurt him sore that he should pay half a crown for the riddance. It was spring time, and Tushy had been sent for urgently, as the rats were eating more food than were the pigs and geese. Tushy arrived with three of his best ferrets, and spent nearly a whole day in slaughter among the pigsties, poultry sheds, stackyard and granary. A pile of dead rats by the stackyard gate was witness to a good day's hunting, and old Dicky rubbed his hands in glee.

'You shall ha' a tankard o' ale for that,' he remarked grac-iously, and Tushy gathered up his ferrets and followed to the house door. He drank the ale, which he found flat and watery,

and waited awhile for Dicky's next move. But Dicky made no
move, so Tushy tactfully inquired:

'What about payment, mister?'

'Payment? Ain't I gi'ed thee a pint o' good ale? What more
does tha want?'

'Half a crown, if you please, sir, and no bother,' was the
reply.

'Half a crown! I'll see thee in 'll first!' growled Dicky. 'I
ne'er heard sich impidence. I'll gie thee a shilling, which is all
the change I've getten by me, and not a penny more.'

'Now look here, mister,' went on Tushy in desperation,
'reet's reet and I ain't hurting yer at half a crown, which is my
usual charge, so pay up and try to look pleasant.'

'Yar saucy rogue! I'll larn yer to talk to me like that! I'll
send for t' bobby if yer don't clear off sharp, that I will!'

'You've no need, mister. I'll fetch him misel, and we'll let
the bobby settle the matter between us, eh?'

'Nah, nah, Tushy, don't do owt rash!' pleaded Dicky, changing his tone. 'We can sattle this little matter wi'out calling the
police. Thou wants half a crown, and two shillings is all I have
by me at present, so if thou cuts thisel a cabbage as thou'rt down
the garden that'll make us straight like.'

Some suchlike pleasant conversation always took place between
the two before Tushy could recover his pay, and then it was
usually a few coppers short. He decided to amend this state of
things, and on this occasion, after vulgarly telling Dicky Drybones
where he might deposit his cabbage, accepted the two shillings
and went home deep in thought.

It was harvest time and Tushy received a message from Common End Farm to the effect that a nest of young rats could be
heard whistling in the meal shed. Tushy answered the call, and
an elfish grin spread over his face as he entered the shed, where
bags of meal were stored for pigs and poultry. Not a ferret had he
brought, nothing but a black leathern bag. He knelt down alongside the sacks of meal, many of them already showing evidence of
rat infestation, and began sucking his teeth. For a while the rat

whistling stopped and all was silent. Then a slight flutter among the sacks, and a monstrous doe rat peeped its nose from between the sacks and looked out. Tushy sucked harder than ever, and the inquisitive rodent came a few inches farther. Tushy's free hand came gently down, gripped the rat by the scruff and placed it in his leathern bag without the rat making any effort to struggle or escape. The animal was completely mesmerized. This Tushy repeated seven times until six half-grown rats and their fond parent lay in the bottom of his bag.

He then called at the farmhouse and asked: 'Are yer there, mister? I've caught yer nest o' rats.'

Dicky came to the door, looked inquiringly at the black bag and said: 'Where?'

'Here,' replied Tushy, 'and afore I kill 'em I wants five shillings.'

Dicky exploded with fury, but Tushy was determined.

'Are yer going to pay up, mister?' he asked.

Dicky refused in most virulent language, whereupon Tushy opened his bag and spilled the rats on the kitchen floor, saying, 'Well, there's yer flipping rats', and made his way home as quickly as possible lest some evil befall him.

Though this did not prove a permanent cure for the old farmer's meanness it saved much future argument, and the old man always insisted on ferrets being used on any future ratting expeditions.

Tushy got well paid too for the nest of rats he introduced into the farmer's kitchen. For several weeks the rats settled down comfortably behind the skirting-board in the farmhouse, until the family could put up with their musical evenings no longer. Tushy was again sent for, along with his ferrets; the skirting-board, not very sound in places, had to be removed and much of it renewed. Tushy's charge for his part of the process was ten shillings, which surprisingly was paid without a murmur.

It was near to Christmastide and Farmer George had invited his friend and neighbour, Frank Smith, to join in the sport of 'rabbiting'. This involved calling on the services of Tushy, who duly arrived at ten-thirty, along with a couple of ferrets. One of the creatures was of a creamy-white colour and one buff with black markings. Tushy picked them up and fondled them with loving care, while they wreathed and twisted their sinuous bodies up the front of his coat in a most obscene manner, at least so thought Frank, who considered them to be detestable creatures. They entered the Horsefield, the hedgerow of which was known to be fretted with rabbit burrows. Tushy put a muzzle on the creamy ferret and placed it down the entrance to a rabbit hole. Presently a rabbit bolted out of a nearby hole and scurried across the field. On the same instant George discharged his gun and the rabbit rolled over on its back.

'Fetch it in, Frank, will you?' asked George calmly.

Frank fetched it in, very much concerned at the role that had been thrust upon him, and his stomach revolted at the whole proceeding. Nine times that morning did he run to pick up a rabbit that had fallen to his friend's deadly aim. On the ninth occasion the rabbit was only wounded and began gyrating in a most distressful manner. Frank hesitated in dismay, so Tushy ran to his aid, picked up the struggling creature by the hind legs and nonchalantly struck it behind the ears with the side of his hand, passing it over to Frank to carry. In so doing rabbit blood had splashed on Frank's boots and gaiters and, gingerly carrying the creature to the heap of dead rabbits, he solemnly vowed within himself that never again would he join in such disgusting sport as a rabbiting party.

'Can we make ten or a dozen of 'em, Tushy?' suggested George, as number nine was added to the list.

'I think so, Mr Western,' replied Tushy. 'I've brought a few nets along, if so be you would like to try along wood side.'

It was impossible to shoot the rabbits if they bolted into the wood, so that in these cases rabbit nets were placed over the holes to prevent them escaping and the rabbits were slaughtered by Tushy's method of a blow behind the ears which dislocated the neck. George preferred to carry on where they were, for he liked to use his gun, so Tushy replaced the creamy ferret in the bag and picked up the brindled beauty. He failed to muzzle the second ferret, deeming it unnecessary; but though they waited quite a while neither rabbit nor ferret made its appearance above ground. Farmer George and Tushy had each brought a spade along with them, and for the next half-hour they were strenuously digging among the thorn roots in search of a ferret that refused to come to the light of day. The ferret was eventually found fast asleep, lying alongside a rabbit with a gaping hole in its neck.

'It must be about noon,' announced George as Tushy placed the blood-gorged ferret in his bag. 'We will have to be satisfied with nine rabbits today, but you must come along with us another day, Frank, and we will try the wood side.'

Frank made no reply, but was confirmed in his resolve never again to be associated with ferrets or rabbits. However, he modified his views and his abhorrence when the following evening he and his wife were invited to a rabbit-pie supper at the farmhouse. He was much against going himself, but as the two women had become so very friendly, using their Christian names of Elsie and Mabel, and as he had been asked to bring along his gramophone, he could not, out of politeness, refuse to join in.

The evening proved very enjoyable, both the musical items and the rabbit pie being in perfect taste and harmony. For the first half-hour they sat before the log fire sipping sherry and discussing events of the day, George dwelling much on the virtues of ferrets to the chagrin of his friend. Then at eight o'clock the two children were called in from the kitchen quarters to partake of the rabbit-pie supper. George and Mabel Western had two little girls, Mary aged eleven and Lillian aged nine, who were in the kitchen with the maid—not because they had been pushed there out of the way, but from choice.

'What would you like to drink?' interposed Mrs Western as the company gathered round the table—tea, coffee or a glass of beer? Frank, perhaps you'd like to try a glass of beer just for tonight?'

'Coffee, please!' replied Frank in alarm at the notion of drinking beer at supper.

'Try a drop of this 3 X, Frank,' advised the farmer. 'We had a fresh barrel delivered this week and I can recommend it.'

So to please his host Frank transferred from coffee to beer, and pulled a wry face at every sip.

'Hah,' breathed George audibly over his pie, 'bit of all kiff, is this. A handy lad wi' ferrets is Tushy, don't yer think?'

'I would imagine so,' replied Frank. 'Supposed to be fierce little creatures, are they not?'

'Depends how you handle 'em,' replied George. 'If they do set their teeth in, there's no way of making 'em leave hold except by throttling 'em off.'

'Here, let me fill your glass up, Frank,' interposed Mabel; 'and for goodness' sake let's have a more entertaining subject than horrid, pink-eyed ferrets.'

She filled up the glasses of the two beer drinkers and, strange to relate, Frank now found the taste to be quite palatable. George returned to the subject of ferrets with renewed vigour, and remarked on Tushy's ability to call the rats to him by the sucking noise through his teeth.

Frank, now beginning to feel courageous and on top of the world, said: 'Sort of sucked in, eh? Now this raises an important issue. Are Tushy's protruding teeth the result of calling his rats to order, or does he call his rats to order because his upper teeth are the way they are?'

This evoked great applause from Farmer George, but his wife remarked somewhat primly: 'Now, children, bedtime, my dears —it's nearly nine o'clock.'

So with a hug and a kiss all round, the two little girls retired.

The grandfather clock had just struck nine when George heaved himself out of his comfortable chair and said: 'Well, you must excuse me for a while—it's time to supper up.'

'Perhaps Frank would like to go with you?' suggested Mabel Western. 'He might like to straighten his legs for a while.'

George lit a paraffin lamp, and the two men went around the

cattle sheds while the two ladies cleared the supper table and did the washing-up. 'Suppering up' was a ritual with Farmer Western; every evening during the winter when the cattle were housed under cover he walked round the yards and sheds, seeing that all was well, and distributing a forkful of hay here or straw there according to requirements. The main place of call was the dairy shed, where a row of matronly milk cows were cudding in somnolent ease. One of the animals was standing on its feet and staring wildly around. It was of a lovely deep red colour, and seemed nervous and frightened in contrast with the rest of the herd which were lying down contentedly.

'A springing heifer,' George announced to his companion, 'a first calver.' He pressed his fingers in the root of its tail and added: 'She'll calve before morning.'

'Does that mean you'll have to sit up all night?' asked Frank.

'Well, I hope not, but one never knows. I'll take a look at her about midnight to see how she's framing.'

Having made everything comfortable the men returned to the house, where they found that the ladies had forsaken the dining-room and were gathered round the hot cooking-range in the kitchen.

'Everything all right?' inquired Mrs Western.

'Janet will calve before morning,' replied George.

'Shall I call Ralph? He's just gone to bed.'

'No, no, certainly not, I'll call him if I need any help, other-wise let him lie—he's been hard at work all day.'

Such was George Western's policy. He never called up his ploughman during the night except as a last resort, though more than once Mabel Western had turned out after the midnight hour to assist her husband over a difficult accouchement in the cow-shed. Mr and Mrs Frank Smith expressed the opinion that it was time to think of returning home, as the hour was nine-thirty, upon which George remarked: 'Nonsense, the night's young yet; you must have a nip of whisky before going out into the cold air.'

There was no gainsaying either George or his wife and, the

D

kettle at that moment simmering on the hob as though in anticipation of such a request, four glasses of hot whisky were soon handed around.

'I don't drink whisky as a rule,' announced George, taking a large gulp which seemed to deny his assertion, 'but it's wise to have a bottle in the house in case a cow needs doctoring.'

'Just listen to him,' broke in his wife, 'trying to make folk believe he buys whisky only to dose poorly cows!'

Thus with pleasant banter did another hour pass by, and it was the alarming hour of ten-thirty when at length the Smiths bid good night to their friends. They were all standing in the doorway saying the final word, when a heart-rending bellow came from the direction of the cattle shed.

'She's on with it,' announced George, and dashed indoors for his lantern. Frank Smith followed him across to the sheds and the two women returned indoors to await developments.

They found the young beast laid on its broadside and moaning piteously. The calf's nose and one foot were protruding. George stripped off his coat, rolled his shirt sleeve up to the shoulder and, methodically and unruffled, thrust the calf's head and foot back into the womb. The heifer seemed more settled and content. George then reached his arm inside the womb, and straightened the unseen foot so that both feet were showing along with the calf's nose. George tied a short rope round the forelegs, and, passing the loose end to his companion, said:

'Pull when she strains, Frank.'

The poor animal bellowed with pain while the men alternately pulled or eased off as the animal strained or rested, until finally the whole body of the calf came bursting out on the bed of straw placed there for its reception. George hastily wiped its nozzle and blew into its lungs the breath of life at which the calf shook its ears and sneezed. Meanwhile the heifer lay panting with exhaustion and seemed almost all out. George dragged the calf up to her nose, which had an electrifying effect. She rose on her knees, making queer, un-bovine noises in her throat, quite outside the accepted language of the cow world. She stood on all

fours, rejuvenated, excited, to lick and mutter endearments to
her first born. One would not have credited a bovine animal with
so much affection.

Her endearments were short lived. The calf was ruthlessly
carried away, and placed in a pen reserved for the new born,
which caused the heifer to set up such a bellowing as filled the
whole shed with reverberating sound. At the end of his unusual
ordeal, Frank found his knees shaking terribly and his brow
bathed in sweat, whereas George remained calm and unruffled
throughout the whole proceedings, moving slowly but purpose-
fully as though the incident were merely routine. They returned
to the house greatly in need of a wash and brush down, and by
the time they had made themselves presentable to Smith's dismay
their hostess had recharged their glasses with whisky.

It was midnight, and Frank, fortified with whisky, cake and
cheese, and feeling somewhat otherworthy, prepared to make
his final departure. He watched his wife and Mabel exchange an
affectionate embrace and, on the principle of 'when in Rome do
as Rome does', gathered the fair Mabel in his arms and implanted
a parting kiss on her cheek. Mabel did not seem to mind in the
least and returned his salute; as for George, not to be left out of
anything, he lifted the demure Elsie off her feet, swung her round
and gave her a resounding kiss which by no stretch of imagination
could be termed a chaste salute.

The Smiths stood for a moment outside their cottage, looking
over the sleeping village and across the valley into the darkness.
At first the night had seemed very dark, with a death-like still-
ness brooding over everything; but as their eyes became accus-
tomed to the change from lamplight they saw that the sky was
full of stars and the row of houses along the village street took
on a definite shape. Likewise the silence became less intense,
and from the low-lying pastures down by the mill came the
plaintive wail of the restless plovers or pewits. Enchanted by
the starlit night, and pleased to find that Night hath her voices
no less distinct than Day, they were suddenly startled by the
hair-raising screech of a tawny owl, a contemporary of Tushy

Whysall the rat-catcher, seeking its supper among George's corn stacks.

'Do you miss the hustle and movement of town life sometimes, love?' asked Frank.

'Not now I have got used to the country, Frank. It's weird to be out on a night like this and yet somehow wonderfully enchanting—not a sound of the day, not the rattle of a cart along the village street, not even the bark of a dog, and everyone except us two night-rakers wrapped in sleep.'

'Not quite everyone,' replied Frank; 'there's a light just appeared in an upstairs window farther down the street.'

'Someone taken ill perhaps. I wonder now who can it be?'

Frank counted the roof tops and replied: 'Mrs Stubbs's cottage. She's rubbing Joe's back ready for work tomorrow. Come along indoors, love, and let's to bed, or we shall need *our* backs rubbing after such a hectic night.'

Nothing disturbed Billy Brunt's irresponsible, easy-going nature. It would be around November time, for Farmer Western was gathering in his potatoes, and Billy's job was to make the potato clamp, or pie, as it is variously called. About half a dozen children, including Quiddy and his eldest sister, had been kept away from school to assist in the 'potato picking', this being a legitimate reason for not attending school. There came a morning when Billy failed to report for duty, to the annoyance of Farmer Western, who saw therein a serious delay in his potato gathering. He had just got his gang rearranged for action, when the gamekeeper came into the field and, after neighbourly salutations with the farmer, remarked:

'Where's your man Brunt this morning, George?'

'Nay, lad, that's what I'd like to know. He ain't turned out this morning, and his lad there says he's poorly.'

'Poorly, eh?' replied the keeper. 'He wern't nowt amiss early this morning when I took four pheasants off him in the Jubilee Plantation.'

'Poaching, eh?' remarked the farmer.

'Seemingly.'

'The silly fool! And what yer going to make of it, Henry?'

'Why, that's what I've come to see yer about, George. I were for takkin' him to t' lock-up, for it ain't first time I've ketched him at it; but knowing as you were busy wi' yer taters and that, and not wishing to make yer short-handed at a busy time, I've called across to see what's best to do.'

'Why, that's good of yer, Henry,' said George, then, turning to his juvenile gang, called out: 'Quiddy, put yer bucket down and come here.' Quiddy, pleased to straighten his back, for picking up potatoes tends towards backache, ran across to the two men and was accosted by his master with, 'Now yer young shaver, off yer go home and fetch yer dad, and don't come back without him, remember! Scoot!'

Some ten minutes later Quiddy returned with his parent, who wore a contrite look for the occasion, and was immediately put under cross-examination by the farmer and the keeper.

'A nice muck-up you've made o' things, ain't yer?' announced George sternly. 'Here's keeper Richards come to take yer away, and I ain't going to stand up for yer. You've let me down for the last time, Billy—weather'll break afore I get my taters up, and if they get spoiled, well, thou needn't come on this farm any more.'

'And it ain't the first time I've caught thee red-handed, as well thou knows, Brunt. And I've my own position to think about wi' the squire, so unless Mr Western thinks it fit for me to be lenient, then it'll ha' to be a court case wi' thee.'

'What possessed yer to go poaching at a busy time like this, yer silly owd fool?' inquired George.

Billy pulled a long face and seemed almost in tears as he replied: 'Why, mester, I didn't think I were doing any harm to nobody, doping a few pheasants; the wife's got a bit behind wi' the butcher, and one o' the bairns has gotten t' croup, so I thought to pull things up a bit afore Christmas.'

'Got one o' the bairns bad, eh?' mused the keeper in a more friendly tone. Young Quiddy, gaping hard at his dad, seemed likewise on the verge of tears, so the farmer ordered him back to his potato picking, and ordered Billy Brunt to get on with his making of the clamp. Then to his friend Frank Smith, who had arrived in the field during the dispute, he remarked, 'Will you empty their buckets into the carts, Frank, until I come back?' and invited the keeper across to the farmhouse for a can of beer.

Frank enjoyed helping on the farm, and as each child filled its bucket with potatoes he exchanged it for an empty one and emptied the full one in a cart that followed along.

'How is your little sister, Quiddy boy?' he asked presently.

Quiddy, glad of an excuse to stand upright, replied: 'Which of 'em?'

'Why, the one that is down with the croup—there's not more than one of them surely?'

'Croup?' repeated Quiddy. 'There ain't nobody at our house gotten t' croup.'

'But I understood your father to say how one of your family was very poorly?'

'Oh, him?' retorted Quiddy with scorn, 'you don't want to take no notice of what my dad says—he says owt but his prayers, and them he whistles.'

Smith was shocked at the callous way in which the young boy spoke of his parent, as also of the way in which poacher Billy had wormed his way out of punishment with the plea of a sick child and a wife who had got a bit behind with the butcher. The general opinion, too, was that young Quiddy was by no means as innocent as he looked and that, like father like son, the young imp of mischief bid fair to finish up on the gallows.

CHAPTER SIX

The Hut

THERE was no doubt about the enthusiasm of the curate to be up and doing, and on seeing what a success the Smiths had made of their gramophone recitals he came forward with the startling suggestion that they built, bought or begged a hut for social entertainment. Frank Smith had been alarmed at the idea and said it could never be achieved in so small a place as Parva, and how the little school held the company very nicely.

'Look here, Frank,' enjoined his reverence. 'When I came down last week there were more people standing than there were sitting, and if we mean to keep things going we must find seating accommodation for the majority of them. Likewise we need a place of our own which can be opened every night, not just occasionally.'

'I agree with you, Gilbert, but how can we get such a place?'

'First of all we must form a committee,' replied Gilbert.

'Lord o' me, how you do rush things, young man.'

'The occasion requires it. Now listen to me, Frank. I've thought it all out; I will come here tomorrow afternoon, and we will go visiting a few likely committee men, such as your friend Farmer Western, for instance. Then there's Mr Robinson—he might be interested, though he's not a churchman. One of them might even have an empty corn or hay chamber that would serve our purpose.'

Frank shook his head, 'I hardly think so,' he replied; 'they both have fairly large granaries, but not with more floor space than we have in the school room. However,' he ended, with a grin at his friend's fervour, 'I'll be pleased to go along with you tomorrow afternoon to see what old George thinks of the idea.'

Accordingly the following afternoon saw the Rev. Gilbert Malham and Mr Frank Smith in search of a quorum of committee men. They found Farmer Western busy in the hay and, after listening to their errand, he agreed wholeheartedly to the idea.

'But', he advised, 'you mu' put it off until the hay be gathered —some time between the hay and corn harvest will suit nicely.'

'Now that's very kind of you, I am sure, Mr Western,' remarked the curate. 'And how are you getting on with it? Have you much hay to gather?'

Although the curate knew George well enough as one of his Sunday morning congregation he knew little about him as a farmer.

George wiped his sweated brow, and remarked, 'One of yer lead t' owd mare on to the next cock', which Frank quickly did, before the curate had time. Then George, while hoisting great forks full of hay on to the cart, remarked: 'We are getting on very well, sir, and if this weather holds, another week should see it all safely in the stack.'

'Splendid,' replied the curate, who didn't know what else to say.

'So long as I get all my hay gathered afore St Swithin's, I shall be happy, sir! Next cock, Frank.'

'St Swithin's, Mr Western?' queried the curate.

'Aye, as yo'll know, being a parson, St Swithin's falls on July 15th, and if it rains o' St Swithin's day, we shall have forty days of it, more or less.'

'St Swithin has been dead these thousand years or more,' remarked the curate, smiling broadly.

'I don't know when he died, sir, though I have heard there was some controversy on where he was to be buried, and as how he, not being satisfied wi' the spot they'd chosen for him, caused it to rain for forty days wi'out letting up, and seemingly he has kept it up ever since.'

Had not his father and his grandfather before him been brought up to the same belief? So how could a young man in his twenties, even if he was in holy orders, alter a decree that had

been in existence for a thousand years. He wiped his brow again
and called out to the man on top of the loaded cart:

'Fill her in and let her go—there's another cart coming.'

The man 'filled her in', then slid off the load to the ground.
Both he and his master were stripped to the shirt and sweating
profusely under the hot sun.

'Hi, bi guy,' said George reflectively as they started on the
next cart, 'after being held up for forty days, I'll wager they'd
put the corpse away wi'out further argument.' Then to Frank
Smith: 'Lead t' owd hoss on, Frank, and the tea should be here
by the time we've loaded this un.'

'Sorry, George,' replied Frank, 'I would like to stop and give
a hand, but Mr Malham wishes to be getting around, and I
promise you a full day tomorrow. There's just one thing before
we go—where shall we meet in committee—at my house or
yours?'

'Why not the school room?' replied George. It'll hold more
folk and you could fix it up now afore the school closes.'

So they bid good afternoon to the farmer, and as the school was
near by called in on Miss Lovibond, the headmistress. A nature
lesson was in progress when they arrived, the last lesson of the
day. Miss Lovibond offered to dismiss her scholars the better
to attend to her callers; but they were insistent that she should
carry on with the lesson as they were always interested in a
nature talk. So they were given a chair each, and listened to the
children recounting, 'what we can see in the countryside at this
season of the year'. Eventually Miss Lovibond mentioned the
ewes and lambs grazing in the pastures. Immediately a boy in the
back row held up his hand, at which Miss Lovibond said: 'Yes,
Willie?'

'Please, miss, I know something else about ewes and lambs.'

'Yes, what is it, Willie?'

'Please, miss, it's in the autumn, about October time, the
farmer smears red-raddle on the tup's breast so that he will know
that the ewes with red-raddle on their backs will have baby lambs
when the spring comes.'

'That will do, Willie Brunt,' replied the teacher, trying to appear unmoved. 'Now, children, put your books and pencils away and get ready for home-going prayers.'

The two men explained to Miss Lovibond the reason for their visit, to which she gave her best wishes, along with permission to meet in committee at some yet unspecified date.

'And now home for a cup of tea,' suggested Frank, 'for I am sure we have earned one.'

'There are more things in heaven and earth, Horatio, than are dreamt of in your philosophy,' says Hamlet, and who shall say Farmer Western was at fault in his assumption concerning the forty watery days following St Swithin's. The weather broke up the week before St Swithin's date, and those who had not gathered in their hay were subject to week after week of more or less continuous rain, causing the hay to lie rotting in the field, with little hope of its ever being worth the picking up. The farm men were put to hoeing turnips in between showers, and looked as bedraggled and dejected as did the haycocks they had been forced to abandon. Owing to the perverseness of St Swithin it was not until one evening in October that a preliminary meeting could be called in the little day school to discuss ways and means of procuring some suitable place for social activities in the village. It did not from the start seem a very hopeful project, for doubts were expressed of anyone wanting social activities after the day's work, and it was doubted if there were enough young folk in the village to merit the expense of providing such a place. However, the chairman, the Rev. Gilbert Malham, was very keen on the project and overruled all objections. Others present at the meeting were Jonathan Keppel, Farmers Western and Robinson, Frank Smith and Miss Lovibond. The erection of a brick or stone building was dismissed as being beyond their present means, which as yet amounted to nothing. It was then moved and carried that Frank Smith be nominated as secretary and treasurer, when, and if, there was anything to treasure. Jon Keppel then came forward with a most helpful suggestion. He had, he said, a hut in one of his quarries which was surplus to his requirements. 'It measure sixty feet by twenty, is in perfect condition, with weather-boarding on the outside and oak-panelling within. My only reason for buying it', he said 'was that it went cheap at a bankruptcy sale.'

'And what price are you asking for it?' queried the chairman, who in spite of his 'cloth' had an eye to business.

'Why, as to price', replied Jonathan, 'I am willing to present it to the cause. It cost me but fifteen quid and so the sacrifice will not be great.'

This offer was gratefully accepted, and the chairman then asked for suggestions as to where to site the hut, looking hopefully at the two farmers, both of whom gravely shook their heads.

Then Jon Keppel spoke again. 'Look here, friends,' he advised, 'I suggest the best site will be on the village green; but before we can erect anything there we must get the permission of the parish council up at Magna. However, this should present no great difficulty, for I have been elected as chairman of Nettle-worth Parish Council for the coming year.'

This information was received with prolonged applause, after which Jon Keppel enlightened them on a few other points of which, in their ignorance of such matters, they were unaware. They would require stone for the foundation of which he had plenty of waste material at the quarry, and which he would be pleased to get rid of free of charge except for carting expenses. Here George Western and Edward Robinson stood up to say they would do the carting, free, gratis and for nothing. Thus ended the inaugural meeting on a promising note to everybody's satisfaction.

The site chosen was a piece of waste ground in the centre of the village. Though called the Green it belied its name as far as grass was concerned. Its surface was all humps and hollows, as though in the remote past it had been quarried, and now it was a wilderness of elder bushes and briars. The first task was to clear away the bushes and level down the hillocks. There was no lack of volunteers, especially from those who had Saturday afternoons free, though little progress could be made during the winter.

But with the lengthening days of spring everyone joined in to erect the hut which was to be their very own. Tom Pippin, the stonemason, gave notable help, laying the foundation, indeed Tom became looked upon as 'foreman on the site'. There were two closed-in stoves which Tom fixed on a cement foundation, one on each side of the room. Saturday afternoon being the main period of activity, the committee considered they had not done amiss to have the building completed in the space of two summers. The response for help was remarkable, everyone in the village coming forward to give a hand, and notably those to whom work had usually no appeal. Billy Brunt came regularly, and proved a hefty wielder of the pick and shovel. Tushy came and did his share, and confided to those concerned that the building would doubtless be pestered with a few rats in course of time, and how he would undertake to rid the place of vermin free of charge.

The high sections of the hut, being too large to be carried on farm drays, were delivered by truck and traction engine belonging to the quarry owners. They were a merry gang who erected those sections along with the struts in place, bolting them securely together, cracking jokes, mostly unprintable, and discussing the current events of the day. The main topic was the famous budget introduced by David Lloyd George, which had imposed a ha'penny tax on their tobacco and would undoubtedly bring ruin to the country. The farmers too were dismayed by the threatened land tax, which would assuredly mean an increased rent for their holdings, with the present low prices of agricultural products, they already had difficulty in meeting it. It was proverbially known that the farmers lived on their losses, though they seemed to do so fairly comfortably. They did not know, neither did masters nor men, that change was in the air, and that the social structure was already cracking at the seams. Within two more years the 'Welsh wizard' was to bring in the National Insurance Act, with the promise of 'ninepence for fourpence' for such as Joe Stubbs, who entertained no great regard for labour, and nothing for the farm labourer who loved to be up and doing.

The men completed their share of the building and then the

women stepped in with soap, water, scrubbing brushes and dusters to put the final polish on the erection.

The official opening took place one Saturday afternoon in May in glorious sunshine. The vicar of Magna had promised to officiate at the opening ceremony, but on discovering a few days before the fixed date that the hut did not belong to the Church, he found to his regret that he had a prior engagement for that day. On that Saturday morning his curate might have been seen peddling down the steep Magna hill, to the imminent danger of dislocating his neck. He burst into Clematis Cottage to give the dire news to his friend, Frank Smith. It was too late now to contact any outsider of note to perform the ceremony, so one of their own members must take over. Who it should be they found difficult to decide, when the curate suggested Mrs Keppel. 'It might be a means of getting her interested in the hut's activities.'

Frank curled his lip and said: 'You can try, Gilbert, and I wish you luck.'

So they called on Mrs Keppel, who, when she saw the curate at her door, received her callers in a most effusive manner. Without any preliminaries his reverence came to the point with:

'My dear Mrs Keppel, we are in an awful fix. As you know, we open our new hut this afternoon and as yet we have found no one to replace our vicar who was to have performed the opening ceremony.'

'Well, my dear sir, what has this to do with me? You don't suppose I can do anything about it.'

'My dear lady,' went on the Rev. Gilbert, 'time is precious, and the occasion demands haste; also of course the opening must be performed by someone of position . . . and charm. Now we know of no one in this village to be compared to you in either of these respects, and so we have taken the liberty of calling to see if you would accept the honour of opening our Community Hut this afternoon?'

'My dear sir,' exclaimed the lady, opening her eyes wide, 'I would be only too pleased to help you in any way I could—but, oh dear me, I have never opened anything in my life. I have no idea what they do on these occasions and I would be quite at a loss what to say.'

'All very simple, my dear, just a few words on the structure of the hut, its purpose and the great need for some such place in our village.'

'Oh dear, it all sounds so easy the way you say it, but I am afraid I would bungle the whole proceedings. Would it not be wiser to choose someone else?'

'Dear Mrs Keppel,' pleaded the curate in a most wheedling tone, 'as I remarked before, it must be someone of importance. Can you, honestly now, think of anyone in this village of more importance than yourself?'

The lady thought awhile without any audible result, then remarked: 'Your reverence will be in attendance, I presume?'

'Certainly, my dear lady, I can assure you of having Mr Smith and myself standing on either side of you to give our support— is that not so, Frank?' To which Frank added: 'Certainly, and if it be any help, I will jot down a few notes to which you can refer in your short opening speech.'

The lady hesitated awhile, then replied: 'You are both so kind that I do not wish to disappoint you, so if you promise to stand close beside me until the ordeal is over, I will accept your invitation.'

Frank and the curate then took their leave, and returned to the cottage, satisfied on a job well done.

The ceremony was an unbounded success. Mrs Keppel, finding herself in distinguished company (for several important people had been invited to be present from town), played her part without too much fluster, though she leaned towards the curate to a greater degree than the occasion demanded. The person most affected by her eloquence was her husband, Jonathan, who stared in wonder to hear his wife declaim (referring to her notes) on the sterling merits of the Brunts, the Whysalls and the Wrigleys. It was a revelation to Jonathan that his wife was acquainted with poachers, rat-catchers and road-sweepers. It was of course all the fault of that wicked Frank Smith, with his helpful notes, for

Mrs Keppel, never having heard of these good neighbours, may have thought them to be farmers or tradesmen in a small way, so that happily no harm was done to her vanity.

The Rev. Gilbert Malham opened the proceedings with a short prayer after which a hearty welcome was given to the visitors. Then Mrs Keppel said her say to the gratification of all present. Tea, sandwiches and a few bring-and-buy stalls followed, which filled in the afternoon's proceedings. About five-thirty the assembly began to thin out, so at six o'clock the curate pronounced the benediction. The effort raised over three pounds, which the committee considered not at all bad for so small a community.

The idea behind the forming of a social club was that there should be no class distinction, that everyone joining should be on an equal footing. On this first occasion, however, the curate was a trifle dismayed to find it was going to be difficult to get cohesion even among the adults, and how Mrs Keppel, Mabel Western, Miss Lovibond and a few of the select visitors had formed an exclusive circle of farmers and tradespeople. It was hoped that this state of affairs would be improved upon as time went on. Frank Smith was a trifle concerned about the two Keppel children, Julia and Val, seated on the end of a form, away from other children. Some of the village boys were eyeing them over in a manner far from sociable, so as a means towards better relationship he called young Quiddy Brunt to his side. Addressing him by his Sunday name he said: 'Now, Willie, you are a boy I can trust. You always strive to do what is right, don't you, Willie?'

'Yes, sir,' replied Willie with a look of innocence on his upturned face.

'I want you to go and sit alongside little Val Keppel and talk to him in a friendly kind of way so that the other boys will not tease him. You understand me, Willie?'

'Yes, sir,' replied Willie in a most gallant manner.

Willie, alias Quiddy, was led to where Val and his sister were seated at the extreme end of a row and looking as though they wished they hadn't come. Unfortunately there was no room to squeeze another person in however small, but in the row behind was an empty seat alongside Farmer Western's two young girls. So Smith coaxed Julia to sit with the farmer's children who, he assured her, were two friendly little girls she would be pleased to know. Julia vacated her seat with ill grace and sat down alongside the Western girls in haughty silence.

At eight o'clock the hut was locked up, and Frank bid a hearty good night to his friend the curate, each of them happy in the knowledge of having performed a good day's work. Finding he had run out of tobacco, he called on Mrs Humble for a fresh supply. She of course wanted to know how they had fared at the hut opening, and it was while he was enlightening the good lady that Quiddy came running into the shop.

'Half a pound o' lard, if you please, Mrs Humble,' he said.

'Half a pound o' lard?' repeated Mrs Humble, then looking in the boy's face exclaimed: 'Why, what's amiss wi' your eye, boy, all black and puffed up like?'

'Bumped it agen suffin,' replied Quiddy shortly, not wishing to discuss the matter further.

'Now you've been fighting agen, that's what you've been doing.'

'Well, it wern't my fault this time,' said Quiddy in defence, adding: 'And my mam's waiting for the lard to rub on me eye.'

Mr Smith joined in to say: 'Quiddy, I'm surprised at you, after all the trust I placed in you this afternoon.'

'And who have you been fighting this time?' asked Mrs Humble.

'It wer' Harry Butcher.'

'Harry Butcher?' repeated Mr Smith. 'But I thought you and Harry were great pals?'

'So we were, sir, until this afternoon.'

'And what happened to cause you to fall out with Harry?'

'Please, sir, he called me a grease-horn, for sitting along wiv Val Keppel, but I didn't take no notice, except to tell him I wer' obeying your orders.'

'And then what?'

'He called you an owd fossil, he did. So I upt, and I gev him one.'

'Oh—er—but you should not have hit him, Quiddy.'

'Looks to me as though Harry Butcher wern't the only one as were hitten!' interposed Mrs Humble, adding: 'And here's yer lard to rub on yer eye—off yer go!'

'That 'ere boy's born to be hung,' remarked Mrs Humble as Quiddy ran out of the shop.

'Indeed I hope not, Mrs Humble,' replied Smith, 'I don't think he's a bad boy at heart—and naturally he felt some resentment towards Harry Butcher.'

'Aye, Mr Smith, and it's a true saying, as often I've heard my old grandmother say, God rest her soul, as you should never nurse resentment, for it's an ill-begotten child that will grow up to bring sorrow to its parents.'

It was found to be impossible to do away entirely with class distinction among the hut membership. Human society is formed of layers, or strata, and the best one can hope for is good fellowship between all classes. As Frank Smith pointed out, one sees it in the school. Most of the boys wear rubber collars which need but a wipe over with a damp cloth to be kept clean, while a certain number of them manage very nicely with a knotted kerchief. An exceptional few wear starched linen collars, but whatever they carry round their necks, they play or fight together regardless of their status symbol. Only later in life do they realize that 'the apparel oft proclaims the man'. As honorary secretary and treasurer of the hut committee Smith found occasion for some alarm that the erection of the hut was not the extent of their expenses. They needed seating accommodation, and though with most institutions such as theirs the cost could be spread over a number of years, the community was so small and so impoverished that the hope of raising sufficient funds in the forseeable future seemed very remote. They scanned the weekly paper for sales of furniture, bought or begged games ranging from dominoes to darts, and formed a small library of

E

which Mrs Smith was voted as chief librarian. Indeed she was the only person in the village capable of filling the position. She was familiar with literature and knew the people, and could advise on which books and authors would be most suitable to their individual tastes. She started a lending library, charging one penny per copy per week, which caused a clash with the curate whose idea had been that everything must be free of charge. He prophesied a falling off in membership but agreed that a modest charge must be made to cover running expenses; and it came to be proved that instead of a decline in members there was an increase, for old and young who had a copper to spare came in for a game of draughts or dominoes, or to borrow a book of such contemporary authors as Thomas Hardy, Mrs Henry Wood, Fenimore Cooper, John Strange Winter or Elinor Glyn, the last mentioned being the author of *Three Weeks*, which Mrs Smith vetted as unsuitable for the village but which was eagerly perused by Mrs Smith, Mrs Western and Mrs Keppel.

It was Mrs Smith's idea too to hold sewing meetings in the hut, and as a means of fostering Mrs Keppel's interest to invite that lady to take the leading part, to which she graciously consented. This involved opening the meeting with a short prayer, which was usually the collect for the preceding Sunday, the lady having no gift for extempore praying. Then, the ladies having settled down to plying their needles, Mrs Keppel would read aloud to the assembly from some improving book from the library shelves. Thus did Mrs Keppel maintain her high position, became friendly towards the cottage wives, and everyone was happy in that state of life into which it had pleased God to call them. For a year Mrs Keppel beamed happily if somewhat condescendingly on her poorer neighbours, when something that was near disaster upset the happy relationship.

It was all due to Sarah Crabthorn, an irritable, contrary old lady, regarded in polite language as 'rather difficult', but in the vulgar tongue as 'owd venom'. She had a moist, glistering eye and an aggressive chin from which could be seen the rudiments of a promising beard. She was troubled with, or perhaps enjoyed, a perpetual sniff, as though she found the atmosphere offensive. They all stood in awe of Sarah, ever censorious of her neighbours, and referred to her, behind her back of course, as that 'old battle-axe'. Mrs Keppel, gaining confidence in her ability as a leader, had conceived the idea of introducing each week some scheme of making a penny go as far as a shilling for the benefit of her poorer neighbours. Mrs Keppel's scheme for this particular day was a recipe for making orange marmalade. Having read out the recipe, she remarked with her usual enthusiasm: 'A splendid idea, don't you think?'

The ladies, being familiar with the making of marmalade in all its variations, maintained a solid silence. Refusing to be discouraged Mrs Keppel went on:

'Now who is going to be the first to try their hand at making orange marmalade?'

Still no reply, until Sarah Crabthorn, after a tremendous sniff, said: 'Bah!'

'I beg your pardon—did you speak, Mrs Crabthorn?'

'I wer' making marmalade afore you wer' takken out o' yer hippen-cloths,' replied Sarah darkly.

'Oh indeed,' remarked Mrs Keppel, trying to appear unperturbed, 'but did you ever try to *sell* the product? That is the whole point of the matter—making enough to sell.'

'And who would I sell it to in this village?' replied Sarah.

'Why, to those who have none of course,' was the reply.

'Not on yer life yer wouldn't, mi lady, not in this village.'

'And why not, may I ask?'

''Cos them 'ats too idle to make their own preserves goes a-begging a jar off them 'ats soft enow to gi' 'em one.'

Here a member of the party whispered confidingly to her neighbour: 'I'm sure I wouldn't like to beg anything off that old battle-axe.'

Unfortunately Sarah's sharp ears caught the remark, which turned her fire completely away from Mrs Keppel to the more hectic assault of personal invective. She turned a baleful eye on poor Mrs Meads and croaked:

'Who borrowed my crimping-irons last week, and they ain't found their way home ag'in as yet?'

'Why, it was you yourself who offered me the loan of them last week, saying I needn't hurry with them as you never used them.'

'And seemingly you ain't hurrying,' croaked Sarah.

At this another member joined in to say: 'Talking about hurrying, Sarah Crabthorn, you ain't in no hurry to return my tatting needles which you borrowed a month back, promising to return them the following week!'

'Now the Lord forgive you, Alice Whysall, for throwing that i' my face afore all the company, for I put 'em away safe i' my cupboard, meaning to bring 'em back the next week.'

An unholy grin spread over the faces of the assembly at Sarah's evident discomfiture. But Sarah was properly nettled and, with all those faces grinning at her, she made one more desperate plunge. 'Anyone can be forgetful at times,' she muttered, then turning her battery full on Alice Whysall she continued: 'We ain't all as smart as your Tushy, Alice, selling rabbits at ninepence, and only allowing a ha'penny for the return o' the skins. Why, everybody knows as how the rag-and-bone man will gi' yer a penny for a rabbit-skin.'

To prevent further rumpus Mrs Keppel rose to her feet and sternly called out: 'Mrs Crabthorn, you must not come here to wash your dirty linen.'

'Dirty linen!' barked Sarah. 'I'd have you know, ma'am, my linen is as clean as yours and better getten up.'

'This has gone far enough,' declared Mrs Keppel, getting really angry. 'I will not stay here to be insulted.' And gathering up her papers prepared to make her departure.

Mrs Smith thereupon in desperation seized Sarah by her massive shoulders, pleading: 'Mrs Crabthorn, will you please leave the room before some mischief is done.'

Sarah gave a sardonic grin, as though greatly enjoying everyone's discomfiture. 'Leave the room, ses you—that I will.' And gathering up the flannelette nightdress on which she had been working in anticipation of keeping herself warm in bed, she delivered her parting shot: 'You won't see me here any more— you've all got yer knife in me, so I'll bid yer good day and yer can kiss . . .'

The bang of the outer door drowned the rest of Sarah's parting sentence, and Mrs Smith, in a matter-of-fact tone though terribly upset, remarked: 'We will now have tea and a biscuit, ladies. Do sit down, Mrs Keppel, I can assure you nothing like this will happen again, for Mrs Crabthorn has resigned from our sewing party.'

Mrs Keppel hesitated. Then, reflecting on her prominent position and her new way of life, sat down and the sewing meeting continued its good work ever after, with a sale of work every year of those garments surplus to requirement, from which the hut funds benefited appreciably.

CHAPTER SEVEN

Alarms and Excursions

ALTHOUGH it was said of Nettleworth Parva that it was a place where nothing ever happened, it did have its moments of excitement. The prolonged rain during the period of St Swithin had caused Dicky Drybones of Common End to gather in his hay on the Sabbath. It was therefore not surprising to the village folk when a few weeks later, after the stack had settled, the whole lot went up in flames by spontaneous combustion.

'It was the judgment of God', said the village folk 'for carting his hay home on Sunday.'

To prove their assertion it was pointed out that none of the other farmers had desecrated the Sabbath and their hay had been gathered in good condition and their stacks spared a conflagration. Another body of opinion shared the blame between the Almighty and two tramps whom Dicky had engaged to help with the haymaking. It was known how Dicky and the two tramps had a violent row when it came to their being paid for their labours, and how the two haymakers hoped his —— ricks would go up in smoke unless he paid them their just dues. So opinion was somewhat divided as to whether it was 'an act of God' or the vengeful antics of the underpaid haymakers. On one point everyone was agreed: 'It served the old skinflint right.' The talk about this startling event revived in the minds of the older generation an even worse tragedy that happened in the district. Beyond Common End Farm is a wilderness of gorse bushes and silver birch trees known as Low Commons, a weird, desolate place, though a paradise for birds: linnets, goldfinches and warblers of every kind. A woman living in a lonely cottage on the edge of the common was found strangled and battered to death there, and to this day the question periodically crops up: 'Who killed Dolly Greaves?'

Suspicion first centred around Pedlar Tim, who used to make periodic visits to the outlying farms and cottages, selling shirts, hosiery, hairpins, safety-pins, collar studs, tapes and tortoise-shell penknives. Indeed there was nothing the housewife might want on the spur of the moment that might not be found in Tim's wonder pack. He was well known around the countryside and well liked for his cheerful manner. He would trudge down many a greasy cart-track to sell maybe a reel of cotton, or even to be told 'Not today mister', all of which he took with a pleasant word and maybe a merry quip.

Wood Cottage stood on the edge of the common. It had originally been a keeper's cottage with a few outbuildings attached and was situated about a mile distant from any public road. It had now been taken over by the Grange farm to house one of its workmen. Tim had never been able to get the present housewife interested in his wonder pack, but he was hopeful, and never failed to call on her when round that way. She was a fair-haired woman with round bright blue eyes and always seemed nervous of having strangers calling at her door. But Tim, ever hopeful, called as usual one morning and found the door slightly ajar. Dropping his pack on the step so that the door could not be closed he called out: 'Any cottons, tapes or buttons?' A startled 'Oh' came from within. Tim peeped inside and saw the woman in the semi-nude hastily trying to hide her lower limbs.

Tim withdrew his head and politely inquired: 'A safety-pin, lady?'

The woman giggled. 'I'm fast for a safety-pin, mister, mi' 'lastic's broke. Lor ain't it funny, you coming and catching me like this!'

'Can't be helped, lady, accidents will happen,' remarked Tim, picking out a card of safety-pins. 'Here, get yersel pinned up lass, afore anybody comes.'

The woman giggled more than ever. 'Afore anybody comes!' she repeated. 'I like that, and who would be likely to come to this god-forsaken hole? Why, anybody could do as they liked wi' me now I'm half undressed and nobody would be the wiser.'

'Come, come, mi lass, thou mus'ny talk so, thou'rt a bonnie lass and tempting to anyone that way given, but it wouldn't do in my line o' business.'

'I guess yer not so innocent as yer make out, mister,' replied the woman. 'Anyway, what pleasure has a woman tied down to a hole like this, and Alf that mean and jealous he never allows me a penny to spend on mi'sel. All he wants me for is to feed his pigs and poultry while he's at work, and to have his meals ready agin he comes home.'

'A sad pity, lass, and you've no family, I reckon?'

'No. Alf says we can't afford no family yet awhile; he aims to take a little place on his own, when he's saved up enough.'

'That's a pity, lass, a babby'd make all the difference to yer living on a lonesome place like this.'

The woman made no reply, but her big blue eyes gazed lustfully on the pedlar. Presently she spoke. 'How about a cup o' tea along with me, mister, there won't be owt wrong in that surely, and Alf won't be in for dinner for another hour.'

'Well, if yer making one for yersel', missis, I'm never against a cup o' tea, was Tim's reply.

The kettle was soon on the boil, the tea was mashed and the pedlar invited to come in and sit down. She seated herself opposite and, with intensity of feeling, remarked: 'I don't care, a woman has a right to enjoy hersel' at times. What pleasure is there to be got here, wi' nowt to talk with 'cept pigs and poultry. And if Alf won't gie me a bab, he mu' take what comes.'

At this point there was a step at the door, and in came Alf, who looked questioningly at the couple seated at his table.

'Lor, Alf, what brings you home at this time o' day?' inquired his wife, hurriedly rising from her chair in a state of flutter.

'We'em going to work in the far field this afternoon,' explained Alf calmly, 'and as it was nigh on dinner time I thought I may as well make my dinner on what I could catch, instead of trapesing all this way from the far field;' then with a fierce look at Tim and at his wife: 'And seem'ly I caught more than I expected.'

'Nothing wrong, mister, and nothing wrong intended,' remarked the pedlar. 'I asked the missis, here, would she brew me a cup o' tea, for which I offered to pay, for believe me that 'ere pack takes it out of a feller on a hot day like this.'

Alf looked doubtingly at the man. 'Well, you've had your drink o' tea, so clear off, and if I catches you in here agen I'll pitch yer out neck and crop!'

'Steady up, mate, there's no need to adopt that attitude,' responded the packman, 'and as for pitching anybody out neck and crop, why, I reckon I'm a better man than you in a rough and tummle.'

'Yer mebbe think so, mate,' growled Alf in a calmer tone, for he knew he was no match for the lively and active pedlar.

Pedlar Tim went on his way, whistling a merry tune, whereupon Alf Greaves turned on his wife in fury. 'What game has you two been up to?' he asked. 'And how long has this carry-on been afoot?'

Instead of making a positive denial of any carry-on, his wife Dolly, cross at being baulked in her attempt at a little lovemaking with the pedlar, replied: 'Yer'd like to know, wouldn't yer?'

'And by God, I will know!' shouted Alf angrily. 'Ain't I warned yer agen having packmen at the door, and here yer a-playing abart wi' Pedlar Tim!'

'And what if I have, yer jealous owd swine! I'll have as many men at the door as I want, and to 'ell with yer and yer niggardly ways!'

He struck her a savage blow on the mouth, to which she retaliated by smashing a dinner plate on his head and the battle began. She spat and scratched at him like a wild cat, until he, in a blind fury, seized the copper-stick and struck her down with a blow on the head. She fell on the sofa, where he gripped her by the throat and shook her until she became blue in the face. There he left her and hurried off to his work. He returned in the evening to find her still there—and dead.

Panic overcame him—he knew not what to do. With some idea

of burying the body on the common he hid the corpse under the dense furze bushes by the corner of the wood.

This tragic event happened in mid week, and by Sunday morning Alf Greaves had not yet acquired sufficient courage to go and dig a grave or even to revisit the spot where his wife lay hidden under the furze or whin bushes. That same Sabbath morning one of the farm lads, a youth of eighteen, took a stroll across the common in the quest of young linnets or goldfinches, both of which found a ready market in nearby Kingsmill. Searching among the bushes he espied a woman's legs and, searching more closely, was horrified to recognize the body of Dolly Greaves of nearby Wood Cottage. He rushed in on the unprepared Alf, gasping: 'Alf, Alf, where's your missis? There's someone lying all dead among the bushes, and I'm sure it's her!'

'Thee mind thi own business, lad, and don't talk so daft!'

'But come and look, Alf, I'm sure it's her! Ony roard, where is Mrs Greaves if that ain't her?'

Alf Greaves tried to collect his scattered wits. 'Look 'ere, mi lad, I'll let thee into sommat. I know thou'rt a sensible lad, and won't let things go no further. My wife's been a-carrying on wi' that 'ere Pedlar Tim and I reckoned they had run away together. If so be as that body i' the bushes is my wife's then Pedlar Tim must ha' killed her.'

'Shall we fetch the police, Alf?'

'Not yet awhile, mi lad—these things want thinking over very careful like. It's plain enough as how Pedlar has murdered our Dolly, but will the police think so? Then ther's yer own neck to think about. Anybody'll know as you ain't done it, but will the police think so? You've getten proper mixed up in the affair, young man, and so long as some'dy swings for it the police won't be partic'ler who it be.'

'But it has nothing to do with me!' protested the youth.

'Ain't it now? That depends which way the cat jumps, mi lad,' remarked Alf enigmatically.

Alf Greaves was eventually arrested in connection with his wife's murder, when he spun a most piteous story of his wife's illicit relationship with the pedlar, and how he had unexpectedly arrived home and caught them together. How he had forgiven his wife and hoped to make it up, but she refused, saying she was going to live with the pedlar. How that evening she disappeared, and he, thinking she had carried out her threat and gone to live with Pedlar Tim, thought that to be the end of the matter.

Pedlar Tim was taken into custody, and under oath recounted all that had taken place on that tragic visit, which hardly tallied with Alf Greaves's account. The proceedings received a check when the chief witness, the youth who had discovered the woman's body, was found to be missing. He had disappeared completely, as though the earth had swallowed him up, after which Alf Greaves recalled how he suspected for some time past that the youth was having an affair with his wife. The proceedings were now adjourned until the youth could be found, which caused quite a stir in the neighbourhood, for he never was found, either dead or alive. A nation-wide search was made; ponds and rivers were dragged, for it was thought that the youth, who was now a suspect of the murder, might have drowned himself. Ports were watched in case he should try to escape abroad, hundreds of people in the surrounding villages were interviewed in hopes of obtaining a clue, but all that was found was a scrap of paper in the lad's bedroom on which was written in lead pencil: 'I never done it. Joe.' The affair became known as an unsolved crime, though everyone was certain it was committed by Alf Greaves, though perhaps not intentionally. He was apparently a dull sort of person—but full of a low cunning. After this affair he became cold-shouldered by everyone, and his employer took the first opportunity to get rid of him. Two years later he left the district and the excitement caused by the murder on the common died down, only to be revived by the excitement of a stack fire.

CHAPTER EIGHT

'Rude Mechanicals'

THE hut thrived beyond the committee's highest expectations, and within a few years was freed from debt, for the sixpences and odd coppers added up surprisingly. The leaders held a meeting in the hut one evening to consider repainting and decorating. They examined the weather-boarding for any sign of decay and were pleased to find everything in perfect order. Secretary Frank Smith and his friends were estimating the cost of painting and decorating, when the Rev. Gilbert, who showed little interest in costing accounts, remarked:

'What we want now, you fellows, is a stage on all that space at the far end which we never use. We could have some splendid performances there.'

'And how much would that cost?' asked Frank, always concerned about the money side.

'What a fellow you are for talking about costs!' retorted the curate. 'Nothing venture, nothing have, my dear Frank.' He was so enthusiastic over the idea that it was agreed to call in a joiner from Magna to give his estimates. As a result a stage was erected, with a small dressing-room partitioned off for the use of the artists, for the reasonable outlay of ten guineas.

During the following winter several short sketches, concerts and gramophone recitals were staged, charging sixpence for adults and threepence for children. Plays were to come later.

The choice of a suitable play took a lot of thinking over, having regard to the talent, or lack of it, in our would-be actors. The Rev. Gilbert insisted that their play should be in rhyme, as being more easily learned by rote, and said that he himself was prepared to write out such a play if a suitable subject could be found. He searched the library shelves, and took away with him a copy of

The Vicar of Wakefield by Oliver Goldsmith, which incidentally had been a popular favourite in the district for some years. The curate returned the book within a few weeks, along with a dozen typed scripts entitled 'Entering Society'. The curate and Miss Lovibond trained the actors to perfection and the play was a great success, particularly the scene where Moses was being dressed ready for the fair. The characters in order of appearance were Dr Primrose, played by Harry Butcher; Mrs Primrose by Doris Meeke; Olivia by Julia Keppel; Sophia by Mary Western; and Moses by 'Quiddy' Willie Brunt. They were all between sixteen and twenty years of age, and Quiddy, now a strapping young fellow of seventeen, was employed in the day time in the local quarries.

A full house was entertained on two evenings the week before Christmas, for many people came from Magna, having heard of the fame of the little community. The admission was one and sixpence (reserved), one shilling the six front rows and nine-pence the rear; 'standing room only', fourpence.

For the scene in which Quiddy as Moses Primrose earned rounds of applause by his superb acting the curtain rises showing Dr and Mrs Primrose seated. A bowl of water along with soap and towels stand on a side table. Moses, seated on a chair, is having his face washed and dried alternately by his two sisters (which to the audience proved uproariously funny):

Moses (*protesting violently*):

    I say, Olivia, leave off, I pray,
    I really need not wash today.
        I'd a real good wash last Tuesday week.
        Oo-ow, you wretch, you are skinning my cheek!

Olivia:

    Now do be quiet, you dreadful boy,
    You are like a child that has lost a toy.
    Really, Moses, I do declare,
    I never saw such unruly hair.

Tugs at Moses' hair, who yells and pushes her away, then tries to
run out. Sophia catches him and hauls him back, saying:

> Come, we must make you fit to be seen,
> Put on this vest of goslin green.
> Come, put it on, and don't be peevish,
> And beware of thieves that look at all thievish.
> Here's your collar, here's your lace,
> Allow me to fix it in its place.

Moses:

> Yow, you've stuck the pin right in my throat!
> I won't be dressed in a silly coat,
> And I won't sell the colt, nor go to the fair,
> Nor will I be dressed like a doll . . . so there!

Throws his lace and ruffles away, and tries to escape.

Mrs P.:

> Moses, I insist, return to your chair,
> And let your sisters comb your hair.
> Is that a pimple, or is it dirt?
> And did you thoroughly air his shirt?

Dr P.:

> My dears, my dears, desist this folly,
> We really cannot sell the colt,
> We have naught to plough alongside Dolly,
> And scarcely can he draw the trolly.
> Besides he looks most melancholly,
> My dears, my dears, desist this folly.

Mrs P.:

> Oh, I could weep with my vexation
> To think you'd spoil our expectation
> Of joining with the upper classes,
> And getting husbands for our lasses.

But I'd have you know, sir, Moses ain't a dolt,
And will bring us home a fortune by disposing of the colt.

Dr P.:

My dearest wife, now do be calm,
The colt is needed on the farm,
To reasoning sound you must comply,
You can't sell a colt that has got a wall eye.
No one will buy a horse that squints,
Has a spavined hock, and lame with the splints.
You'll find them otherwise engaged,
When you show them a horse half blind and aged,
My dears, I beg you listen to reason,
We will keep the colt for another season.

Olivia:

Oh, Papa, after all our care
In dressing Moses for the fair,
Is this the end of our endeavour?
(Sobs.) And dear Lady Blarney thought us awfully clever,
Now we must stay here for ever, and ever.
    Then pen these lines for me when I am gone,
All for the sake of a horse that was aged,
She missed her chance of becoming engaged,
    Olivia Primrose, aged twenty-one.

Moses:

Dear sister Olivia, if you feel like that
I withdraw my objections. Reach me my hat,
You may have your chance of entering society,
And choose a rich husband from among the variety.

Sophia (leads Moses forward):

There, how nice to have all so amicably settled,
Though Papa still seems inextricably nettled.
I think he's now ready in all main essentials,
So Moses step forward and show your credentials.

Dr P.:

> Excuse me, dears, I was not aware
> We were disposing of Moses at the fair?

Moses:

> They'd dispose of anything moving on legs
> For the sake of Lady Blarney and Caroline Skegs.
> So if you have finished messing my hair
> I will see you all later, after the fair.
> *They all follow Moses out wishing him farewell.*

There could be no doubt as to the success of the first venture into dramatic art, and as the crowd surged through the doorway, most of them to be carried away by car, cycle or on foot to neighbouring Magna, the curate was seen to kneel in thankful prayer that the Community Hut was fulfilling its purpose. Frank Smith watched the crowd pressing through the one and only exit, and a horrible fear possessed his mind. Suppose the hut caught fire when filled with people, with only one door through which to escape except for a small door beyond the stage? He broke into a sweat of apprehension and hastily called a meeting of his colleagues. They were but mildly interested and, while admitting the advisability of having two emergency exits, accused Frank of being too sensitive to the danger. Nevertheless two emergency exits were cut in the sides before ever another play was put on.

One remarkable sight that evening was Mrs Keppel pausing to shake hands with Quiddy and commend him on his wonderful performance. How that woman has changed since having something to occupy her mind! As she shook hands with this fine young fellow did she associate him with the vulgar little imp who one day struck her darling Val on the nose?

The audience having gone their way home, the artists were regaled with coffee and cakes, and everyone was in high good humour as they discussed the performance and speculated on performances yet to come. They were applauding each other

sky-high, when the puckish curate brought them back to earth
by quoting the lines from *A Midsummer Night's Dream*:

> 'A crew of patches, rude mechanicals
> That work for bread upon Athenian stalls.'

The 'rude mechanicals' lingered on the roadway as though
loath to depart from the precincts of their beloved hut.

Julia Keppel, now chatting amicably with everyone, still
carried that air of aloofness she had as a child. Perhaps it was her
more refined speech in sharp contrast to the village idiom, that
made one judge her as being proud and haughty. Nevertheless
she was heard to remark, as they stood on the roadway:

'I say, Quiddy, do you mind seeing me home? It's pitch dark
and I'm scared to death of bogies. Daddy, Mum and Val will have
been home ages ago.'

'Right, Julie, Olivia Primrose,' replied Quiddy gaily. 'I will
be thy guide and free thy path of bogies, bats or blackbeetles.'

Julia thrust her arm in his as they turned in the direction of
The Cedars. Presently she remarked:

'Quiddy, if you were a gentleman you would ask to be allowed
to carry my case.'

'Sorry, Julie, give it here,' replied Quiddy.

'Oh, Quiddy, I wish you were not so rough spoken,' sighed Julia.

'How yer mean, Julie?'

'There you go again. Do you know, Quiddy, I like you ever so
much.'

'Thanks, my dear, it's the first time I've ever heard of anyone
liking me.'

'Silly—all the girls in the play love you.'

'Goodness me, there's no accounting for taste, is there?'

'Now do be serious, please. I like you very much, Quiddy.
Do you like me?'

'Heaps a lot, Julie,' he replied, giving her arm a squeeze.

'But of course I could not marry you.'

'Nobody axed you,' retorted Quiddy, trying to release his
arm.

F

'There, now you are cross,' said Julia, clutching his arm. 'What I mean is you are not educated, nor well brought up, and Mother will expect me to marry someone well educated, and if not wealthy, at least talented, though of course you proved tonight that you are not without talent.'

'The talented young Irving marries the heiress of a wealthy quarry owner,' mocked Quiddy.

'There, now you are making fun of me, and I do not believe you care for me the least bit.'

'I do, Julie, I really do, I've never met anyone I like better than you,' asserted Quiddy, now getting warmed up. 'I suppose it's with us rehearsing together this winter, but what's the use?'

They walked along in silence for a while, then Quiddy broke in: 'I say, Julie, did yer mean it? If I wer' better educated, made my mark and that, would you consider—that is, could we be better friends?'

'Quiddy dear, we will always be good friends, I hope, whether you become another Henry Irving or not.'

'I have no wish to become an actor—not for a living, remarked Quiddy. 'Listen, Julie, I believe I have another talent, better than acting; and, talking of talents, reminds me of what old Robinson said to us once at our Sunday school anniversary. I've never forgot it, though I were only a kid at the time. He said as how the man with only one talent was as important as the man who had five talents. That what mattered was what yer did with them, not how many talents you possessed.'

'But that's ridiculous, Quiddy. It tells you plainly in the Bible that the man with one talent had it taken away from him. But here we are at the gate, and it's been a lovely walk home in the dark.' She squeezed his hand. 'Good night, Quiddy dear.' And she passed through the iron gate. She closed the gate, then paused. 'You may kiss me if you wish, Quiddy,' she whispered. 'Just one.' She placed her cheek to the iron bars, then ran up the drive without further word.

Quiddy turned his steps towards home, his head in a whirl of emotions. It seemed incredible that this could have happened to him and that he had actually kissed the lovely Julia—and at her own invitation. His supper was waiting when he arrived home, and his mother greeted him with: 'Where yer bin while now? The play wer' over above an hour back.'

'We stayed to have coffee and chatted awhile,' replied Quiddy, drawing up to the table.

Billy Brunt senior, seated by the fire, broke in to remark:

'He ain't a bairn no longer, lass—a young feller has a reet to a bit of a spree now and then.'

'A bit of a spree!' retorted his wife. 'Just look at the face of him, at his eyes now. He's bin having a bit of a spree all right. What yer had to drink, I'd like to know.'

'Coffee and nothing else, Mam,' replied Quiddy shortly.

'Coffee?' repeated Dad with amused scorn. 'Arter the way you and them two lasses were towing one another around I'd ha thowt ye'd ha' wanted sommat better na coffee.'

'A stuck-up piece that Julia Keppel if ever there was one,' commented Mam.

'Oh, I donno,' replied Dad. 'It's just the way of her. A rare bonnie gal sho' growd into.'

Meanwhile Quiddy got on with his supper, stirred by strange emotions. He even resented his parents discussing the name of Julia, as though it were an unwarranted liberty on their part. He noticed the stains on the tablecloth and the general untidiness that prevailed in the room. He was aware too that his father, though good-natured and nobody's enemy but his own, was noted for his poaching proclivities, and all these things formed an unsurmountable barrier between himself and his friendship with Julia.

'Haughty young madam that there Julia Keppel, like her mother—stinks o' pride!' announced Mrs Brunt, suddenly breaking in on Quiddy's thoughts.

'Mam,' replied Quiddy, rearing up. 'I wish you'd leave Julie's name out of it. You have never spoken to her in your life, so you can know nothing of her, good or bad.'

'Don't you speak to me like that, mi lad,' retorted Mam, 'or I'll box yer ears, big as yer are!'

'Ho-ho!' remarked Dad, grinning widely. 'Aiming high, ain't yer, boy? Juliet Keppel, bi guy! Now, for mi'sel I would ha' preferred Mary Western, a nice bit o' farmland wi' a bit o' rabbiting thrown in, but e'ery one to his taste!'

Quiddy refused to be further drawn in and finished his supper in silence. He pushed back his chair, took off his shoes and stood in his stockinged feet by the stairs door.

'Mam,' he said, 'would yer mind very much if I left home?'

'Now, what's takken yer? What yer want to leave home for—ain't my vittles good enow?'

'It isn't that, Mam, I thought I might better myself if I took a job away from home.'

'After all I've done for yer, bringing yer up and that!' exclaimed Mam, warming up; 'then when yer can be useful wi' yer seven and sixpence a week yer want to leave home.'

'You won't be any worse off, Mam, I promise you that,' replied Quiddy. 'I can send you a few shillings each week, especially if I get a job with more money, and you won't have me to feed.'

'Well, there ain't much choice o' work if he stops here,' agreed Dad, 'and I don't blame the lad for leaving home if he wants to get on. I hope he remembers his dad when he's made his fortune and, like a dutiful son, treats him to a jar now and then for having brought him up respectable.'

'It's that Mr Smith who's at bottom o' this,' went on Mam, 'putting idees into yer head, wi' high-falutin notions what's above yer own station in life, and me working and slaving my fingers to the bone to bring yer up clean and tidy, and then to be sarved like this.'

Mrs Brunt may have brought her family up fairly clean and tidy, but to say she had worked her fingers to the bone in the effort was a gross overstatement.

CHAPTER NINE

The Adventures of Joe Wrigley

FRANK SMITH had occasion to call in Mrs Humble's shop one day, and found the old lady beaming over with joy and happiness.

'May I have a private word with you, Mr Smith?' she asked.

'Certainly,' was the reply. 'What is it, Mrs Humble?'

'Well, I aim to get married come Whitsun, and I wondered if you would run me up to Magna, you and Mrs Smith, and stand witness at the registry office.'

Frank stared in dumb amazement. Could the old lady be serious or was this some joke she was trying on? She smiled at his bewilderment, and said: 'Well?'

Recovering his speech Frank said: 'Yes—yes, of course, if you really mean it, Mrs Humble.'

'I've meant it for years, sir, but wouldn't give consent while Father was alive.'

'And who is the happy man?' inquired the incredulous Frank.

'It's Joe—Joe Wrigley the roadman. I've knowd Joe for years—afore ever he came to Parva, I've knowd Joe.'

They were married at the registry office in Magna, Joe saying 'he didn't want no fuss', and the reception was held in Mrs Humble's front parlour, where the few invited friends beheld a newly transformed Joe. For those who had always seen him with brush and shovel and dressed in corduroys it was difficult to associate this chubby, red-cheeked fellow in navy-blue serge, sporting a pink carnation in his buttonhole, with the familiar figure of their roadman. They had a real slap-up wedding feast of Mrs Humble's best ham, followed by the customary wedding cake and port wine. There were eight guests, all particular friends of the happy couple, who toasted them and wished them many years of happiness together. Then, the main celebrations being over, Mrs Joe Wrigley, formerly Humble, seeing her guests settled comfortably, each with liquid refreshment according to taste and cake *ad lib*, gave a short preliminary to Joe's story.

'I first knew Joe when he were a hired lad living at The Grange, and I wer' the servant gal there. We had walked out together once or twice, but nothing serious, for we were both young, and there was plenty o' time. Well, you will have heard o' the murder 'at took place at Wood Cottage, and how Alf Greaves, the husband, and Pedlar Tim were at first suspected, and were took away to be tried; how it was then discovered as one o' the farm lads was missing, and so the case was held up until the lad could be found, and that same lad was Joe, sitting there as ever was. And now, Joe,' she added, turning to her husband, 'what happened. Tell us all about it.'

'Why, it's sommat I don't care to talk about,' replied Joe, 'and I reckon it's best to be forgotten.'

'Nonsense, Joe, come along now,' demanded the bride in a manner that showed she was starting her wedded life in the manner she intended to go on.

'Why, I set off on t' wrong foot for a start,' began Joe. 'It were me what found Dolly Greaves's body among the bushes that Sunday morning, and o' course I'd nothing to do wi' the affair, and had no need to ha' run off as I did. But Alf Greaves persuaded me, said the police would be sure to suspect me for having a hand in his wife's murder, and I should be tried, and whatnot, and the best thing for me to do was to run away until the affair had blown over. I says: "I ain't done nothing, and I ain't going to run away." Says Alf: "Now look thee here, thou art nobbut a lad as yet, and doesn't understand these things. I know thou hasn't done it, 'cos it were that Pedlar Tim, but he's fly, and if he can wriggle out of it they will come for thee. Now if you lay hidden somewheres until the case has blown over, you can come back again when they've hung the pedlar, and all will be well." I soon found out what a mess I'd let mi'sel into, but Alf kept on with his blarney, and I wer' so scared and bewildered by what

I'd found in the bushes, that I ran away that same night after leaving a note in the bedroom.

'At first I decided to make for my home village near Malton in Yorkshire, but realizing that if the police came after me they would call at my home, I altered my tracks. I managed to get a job haymaking on a lonely moorland farm and was glad of it, for I was beginning to feel peckish. Also I felt safe there and, apart from feeling what a fool I'd been for running away in the first place, could ha' settled down nicely with the farmer. Then one day he had been to Bakewell market, and when he came home he started eyeing me over in a strange manner and asked: "Where did yer come from, young feller, afore you arrived here?"—"Malton, up i' Yorkshire," I says, wondering what wer' coming next. "Sounds likely," he says, "judging by thy speech." He then went on to say: "I were reading a newspaper down i' Bakewell about a murder somewhere ower by Kingsmill, and how the police wanted to know the whereabouts of a farm lad they wanted to interview about the case. They had issued a description o' the youth, and I thought, by gow, it might be you. But it could na' ha' been you, for yer a decent lad as I can see." He then eyed me over harder than ever and ses: "But I shall ha' to report thi' to the police 'cos the paper said so, and as we've about finished the haymaking I may as well pay thee up now."

'I eventually landed i' Sheffield. I felt safe in a busy city, for there were that many folk running about it seemed unlikely as anybody 'ed notice me. I got a job carting coke to some big works, and everything wer' going all reet when one Saturday night I called in a public house for a pint o' beer. The room wer' crowded wi' forge men and such, who were discussing the news in the evening paper. A great burly forge man read out, "Police notice. Five pound reward will be paid to any person who can give information as to the whereabouts of Joseph Wrigley", followed by a description of mi height and the way I was dressed. I was proper scared when that forge man sitting next to me clapped his great hand on my shoulder and says: "By gum, matey, five quid! That ed keep us in ale a month o'

Sundays." I felt as though everybody i' the place were staring at me, and soon as I could wi'out calling attention I went out, though 'o course nobody in the pub were taking any notice o' me. Their opinion o' the reading was that the farm lad had committed the murder and had now drowned himself rather than face up to it.

'I were reet miserable after I left the pub, not knowing which way to turn, and calling mi'sel no end o' names for letting Alf Greaves persuade me to run away. I reckoned, too, that having run away and drawn suspicion on mi'sel I couldn't very well go back and gie mi'sel up. I travelled westward, after buying mi'sel a pair o' moleskins and a blue slop so as to look more like a navvy than a farm lad, and when I reached Macclesfield I ran across a fellow by the name o' Pincher, who said he was making for Manchester. We pal'd up together, or rather he pal'd up wi' me, for I wer' that miserable I didn't want to pal on wi' anybody. The strange thing about Pincher was that he was never short o' a copper, or even a bob, while I was always down to my last penny. We stayed a week or two i' Manchester, where I managed to collect a copper or two, holding 'osses or doing odd jobs. Then one day he suggested we should try Liverpool for a change, as Manchester was getting too warm for him. I couldn't understand that, for I was feeling anything but warm living on a mug of cocoa and a slice of bread and fat, if I wer' lucky. He wer' a wrong 'un, wer' Pincher, but I didn't know that till later. It wer' our first night i' Liverpool, when the bobbies called at our lodge and fetched Pincher out o' his bed. My—I wer' never so scared in my life, for I wer' sartin sure it wer' me they had come for.

'After that I wandered about Liverpool for the rest of the winter, getting an occasional job at the docks, and by and by learned the ins and outs o' things from the reg'lar dockers. When spring came I managed to get taken on as cabin boy on a boat, and worked my passage to Montreal. Though I felt safer on t'other side o' the watter, I wer' far from comfortable. I had nowhere to go and nobody seemed inclined to give me a job. I hid in a freighter that was bound for Winnipeg, having heared it was the likeliest place to find a job on a farm. I asked several people who wer' unloading their goods off the train if they could find me a job, but most of 'em wer' in too big a hustle even to answer. I were near to crying wi' misery, when a farmer called out for me to give him a hand with a large packing-case. After I'd helped him to loaden up I asked him: "Could yer find me a job for the summer, mister?"—"Why, I got plenty of help,' he says and gave me a dollar. I must ha' been looking down i' the mouth, for I wer' feeling lost in a strange country, when the farmer's wife remarked: "Poor kid, let him get up behind, John—we shall never miss his vittles."

'I stayed twelve years with John Maynard and his wife, and a better home I couldn't wish for. They treated me as one of the family. They had three sons and one daughter, the eldest boy being fourteen and the little gal a mere toddler. As the sons grew up and able to work on the farm, I expected my service would no longer be required. But no mention of my going was ever made, though the family, including myself, often discussed together a hope that Jack, the eldest, would eventually set up on a place of his own. But they were a close knit sort o' family, if you understand what I mean, and when a holding did become vacant it was either too far away from home or failed to suit somehow or other, and the while I was there there was no break in the family circle.

'Then one day—it were the twelfth summer o' my being wi' the Maynards—a tramp feller called, a hobo we called 'em, begging a drink o' watter and a crust o' bread if we'd one to spare. A proper down-and-out he looked, and the picter o' misery, sitting there on the mounting block gulping down his plate of hot mash. Catching sight o' me standing in the doorway, he stared long and hard till his eyes seemed like popping out o' his yed. I didn't like the way he stared and, walking across to him, I ses: "What's up mate, does tha think tha'll know me next time?" It wer' Alf Greaves, reet enough, though I would ne'er ha' recognized him if he hadn't ha' spoke. Wi' a look o' terror in his face he blurted out: "Joe—Joe Wrigley, ain't it?"

'I called for Mrs Maynard to come and she and all the family came out, and when they heared who he was the lads were for knocking of him out there and then. The Maynards had known my story for years, for they were not the sort o' folk from which one would withhold a secret. John Maynard was for handing the fellow over to justice there and then, but I prevailed on him to let the poor feller go, as I could see no useful purpose in having the poor wretch hung after all these years, seeing that my life had been all happiness and contentment, while Alf, by the look of him, had spent the time in misery. It wer' Mrs Maynard who had the last word. She gets a sheet o' paper, and makes Alf write out a confession, proving my innocence, and how it was he himself who had throttled his wife that day in a fit of jealousy. Evidently finding every man's hand against him he had sought refuge abroad, but found to his sorrow that his conscience had followed him.'

Pausing to take a generous drink at his beer, for Joe preferred beer to any fancy drinks, he continued with his story:

'After the harvest was gathered in I decided to come home to England to prove my innocence according to Alf's confession. Likewise, I'd a longing to see the old folks agen if so be they were still alive and living near Malton Strange', went on Joe, in a low voice as though talking to himself, 'how some things sticks i' one's mind. I wearn't short o' money, for Mrs Maynard had reg'ler put a bit i' the bank in my name, God bless her good heart. It wer' the hour o' parting, what brought a lump to the throat, and made us act like unweaned bairns.

'Missis kissed me goodbye wi' tears in her eyes, and hoped I would come back; if not I must write to them regular, which I did for a time, but being no scholard I soon forgot. Shaking hands wi' the menfolk wern't quite so mellow like, though they wished me god-speed and hoped to hear good news of me. It were Anne, now a sweet and comely creeter o' seventeen, who made us all pipe the eye. Anne, now growd up, and hanging on my neck just like when she were five and I had to tuck her in bed 'cos she wouldn't allow no one but her Joe to do that, and who had to play with her toys and dollies on the har'stan on long winter nights. She made me promise to come back after I'd seen my own folk in England, though I knew I never would, for Anne wer' not yet eighteen and I wer' turned thirty.'

'Well, that's a corker,' broke in George Western as Joe paused again in his story. 'Fancy our old road-sweeper having travelled all that far, and us thinking he had never been separated from his wheelbarrow.'

'Aye, but he ain't finished yet,' broke in his bride, now Mrs Joe Wrigley. 'Come on, Joe, what happened next?'

'Why, first of all', began Joe, roused into action, 'I made for Yorkshire to visit the old folk if so be they were still there and alive, but they had left the village some years before. No one knew what had become of them, only that some scandal concerning one o' the lads had caused the family to leave the district and to settle down in some place where they were unknown. I drifted my way back as far as Magna, thinking mayhap I might light across Lucy there, who were the sarvant lass at The Grange in my time and who were the only body I knowed around here. My aim was to prove my innocence wi' the bit o' paper I carried, and I hoped, if I came across Lucy, she might gi' me a hand that way. I had plenty o' money by me for present needs, and I ain't a malicious sort o' person, and I looked at it in this way. The affair was now almost forgotten, and if ever the case should crop up agen—well, I had Alf's confession in my pocket, so let sleeping dogs lie, I says.'

Joe paused again, at which his wife took up the story in more rapid style than Joe's slow and measured speech.

'Joe called in my shop one day for an ounce o' twist tobacco, and I says to myself, I seem to know that face, for it ain't often one meets a stranger in Parva—then it came to me all in a flash. "Ain't you Joe Wrigley, mister," I says, "what used to live at Grange Farm?"—"That's as may be, missis, but how do you know?" says Joe. So I explained as how I were the servant-gal who he used to know, after which Joe explained as I were just the person he was looking for and showed me the paper he carried about with him. I agreed with Joe about letting the matter drop and after a time persuaded him to leave the confession with me, so that it would neither get lost nor defaced by his carrying it about. Joe eventually got a job on the council as roadman at Parva, where he's been these many years, and I managed to get him that little one up and one down cot, which were but a hovel, but did until now, when he can share a comfortable home along o' me.'

Another of the guests, after listening in silence to Joe's strange story, remarked: 'Is it not strange that no one except you, Mrs Humble, to use your old name, ever recognized the returned Joe?'

'Not really,' was the reply. 'Joe never visited this village during his stay at The Grange. The people who live over that way do their shopping at Kingsmill, which is much nearer.'

The wedding guests learned too how Lucy, then a young girl, had eventually wed a young farm hand named Walter Humble. Their wedded bliss was brief, for within two years Walter was rushed to hospital with a stoppage—what is now known as 'appendicitis'. An operation proving unsuccessful; the young widowed Mrs Humble went to live with her aged parents, whom she nursed until the last of them, her father, died last year, and she could conveniently take on Joe. Such was the story to which the guests were entertained at the wedding of Joe and Lucy Wrigley.

CHAPTER TEN

The Calm before the Storm

THESE occasional ripples of excitement show up even on Parva's placid duck-pond, though, following Dicky Drybones's burnt-out haystack, Lucy's wedding and Joe's strange adventures, Parva became as becalmed as a 'painted ship upon a painted ocean'. However, the hut continued to fulfil its useful purpose, and after the harvest had been gathered in the Rev. Gilbert called a meeting concerning another play he wished to produce during the coming winter for the delight and edification of the community. To everyone's dismay Quiddy was missing—had been for some while, though during the summer months his absence had not been so noticeable. Jonathan Keppel was asked whether the boy was still engaged in his quarries. Jonathan had looked puzzled at first, then replied: 'Oh, that lad of Brunt's—he's been left some while ago.'

'Was he dismissed or did he leave of his own accord?'

'There was nothing wrong, I rather liked the lad—a good worker and all that. You'd be surprised if you knew why I parted with him. I found out that during his dinner hour the lad was cutting out figures on slabs of stone—nothing great, just ivy leaves and floral designs—but I could see he knew how to use a sculptor's chisel, so I decided to give him a chance. I happen to know a monumental mason with whom I sometimes do business in dressed stone, so I persuaded him to take young Brunt into his employment. Simple as that it was. That young fellow has talent and should do well for himself.'

This was pleasing news, though the hut had lost its star performer. However, 'the play's the thing', and the company continued to perform under the able leadership of the Rev. G. Malham, Mr Frank Smith and the school ma'am, Miss Lovibond.

93

Apart from the social gatherings the village pursued its calm, unhurried way, seedtime and harvest and the daily routine that had gone on unchanged through past generations, and would remain so throughout all generations to come.

Among the 'off-beat' activities of the farmer's year was the cleaning out of the pigeon-cote. This was an annual event, and the pigeon dung, being dry and powdery, made an excellent fertilizer for the turnip land, being sown on with a tillage drill along with the turnip seed. Farmer Robinson had a pigeon loft, a brick structure interposed on top of the coach house. One reached it through a trapdoor in the coach house roof, and on the annual clean-out any vehicle within was taken out and a farm cart or wagon placed under the trapdoor. What a pother among the pigeons, and what a smell when the trapdoor was opened! The interior walls were a fretwork of pigeon holes with a protruding brick on which the birds settled to get on their nests. There must have been hundreds of pigeon holes and hundreds of pigeons, some sitting tight on their nests in spite of disturbance, though most of them had fled for safety on the outside roof. Most of the birds were of the homer variety, a bluish colour, though there were tumblers in brown and blue, and fantails dressed in purest white. It was a stuffy, undesirable job, cleaning out the pigeon loft, when the dung had formed a covering almost a foot in thickness and had to be shovelled into the wagon standing below, and the men were always glad to get it away to the field into God's clean fresh air.

There were the nests to be cleaned out too, eggs and unfledged squabs destroyed, lest the pigeon population should become redundant, and any young pigeon of table size was claimed by the men as a sort of perquisite. Pigeon fliers would doubtless be horrified to think of their pet fancies receiving such cavalier treatment as the farmer's pigeons did on their annual spring-clean.

The years passed happily away, with no indication that our pleasant little backwater would ever be otherwise than a peaceful and contented spot where nothing ever happened. True, since the founding of the hut, and owing to the efforts of the curate in staging a play each winter, the place had become better known, and some impudent person had built a glaring red-brick bungalow in the village which was quite out of keeping with the grey, stone-built cottages; but apart from that there was no visible sign of change.

As everywhere, youth grew into manhood, evidenced by Ralph the plough lad being seen walking out with Bessie, the maid at The Cedars, across the common on Sunday evenings. This showed some change in Mrs Keppel's attitude to her maid, for in the past there had been a strict rule at The Cedars of 'no followers' among the domestics. Perhaps the good lady was considering her own daughter, for Miss Julia was growing up too, and like all mothers Mrs Keppel hoped some day to make a suitable match for her one and only daughter. Never deeming it likely that Julia might wish to pick and choose for herself, she had encouraged a young solicitor from Magna to pay his respects. It is said that 'the course of true love never did run smooth', but what a rough passage it is when the love is all on one side. Julia detested the fellow and rejected his advances with scorn. The persistant lover refused to be discouraged and, aided and abetted by Julia's mother, popped the question. Julia laughed in his face and blandly told him that if ever she married it would be to a man and not a white rabbit—a reference to the man's very fair hair.

Mrs Keppel pleaded in vain to her daughter to be reasonable, saying: 'Percival is a young man of wealth, breeding and position, a most suitable match in every way. You stupid girl, what more do you want?'

'Quiddy,' was the reply. 'Mama dear, if I ever marry it will be to Quiddy, otherwise William Brunt.'

Which same foolish assertion caused quite a furore at The Cedars and Julia was in dire disgrace.

There are other detractions and attractions at The Cedars, and no one can forsee what will be the outcome of it all. The son, Valentine, has quite grown out of his babyish ways and has developed into a fine young fellow, though of somewhat slender build. To the disappointment of his sire he takes no interest in stone but bestows all his affections on the soil, to which end he has renounced any intention of becoming a quarry owner and hopes one day to own a farm. He has engaged himself as spare man at Wheatlands, and works alongside Ralph and the other farm men at the multitudinous jobs of agriculture. He has long been a member of the curate's troupe of players where he became acquainted with Mary Western, so whether Mary had any influence on his decision to desert stone for soil is just a matter of opinion.

Thanks to the efforts of Tom Pippin in rectifying the garden at Clematis Cottage the Smiths' rose-bed is a joy to behold. Roses of all the newest varieties, along with the old moss rose, Tom had tended with loving care, and this year persuaded his employer Frank Smith to enter some of the choicest blooms at the Kingsmill Flower Show, to be held in July. Everyone pauses to admire the blooms when passing by and recently someone must have paused longer than admiration requires, because on the morning before show day, when Tom went to view his treasures, all the best half-opened blooms had gone. Consternation reigned in the cottage, and Tom swore fit to blight every rose in the garden. He knew who'd done it, he said, and vowed vengeance on the culprit in unmeasured language. But the fine blooms were gone and there was nothing one could do about it except grin and bear it. It was a warm day of brilliant sunshine and, the hay being safely gathered into the stack and the corn not quite ready for harvesting as yet, Farmer Robinson, his wife and daughter, Miss Harriet, decided on a trip to the flower show at Kingsmill in the pony and tub. There was a sale of produce after the show and Miss Harriet, attracted by the lovely roses, bought a prize-winning bunch to give to her friend and neighbour, Mrs Lucy Wrigley, at the shop. It was late when they arrived home and the shop was closed, so Miss Harriet took the bunch of flowers home, placed them in a bowl of water, then, struck with a brilliant idea, said: 'I know what I will do: I will take the bowl of roses and place them on the shop doorstep straight away. Won't Lucy get a surprise when she opens the door in the morning!'

Tom Pippin, walking along the road in the early morning, stared in surprise to see a bowl of roses on Mrs Wrigley's step.

'Now how come they to be there?' he asked himself, and recognized them to be the missing blooms from Frank Smith's garden. While he stared in wonder, the shop door opened, and Joe Wrigley peeped out. Tom bristled up and, coming nearer, said: 'Hi, Joe, what's bin going off? I'm surprised at thee, I thowt tha could keep thy fingers clean.'

Joe looked questioningly at his interrogator, then, noticing the rose bowl for the first time,' exclaimed: 'Eh, bless me, what ha' we gotten here? Roses, bi guy!'

'And how came you by them there roses, Joe? I thought it wer' some'dy else, but apparently you wer' the thief.'

'Thief, Tom! What yer mean?'

'Nah, don't come it wi' me, Joe, some'dy pinched Smith's roses day afore yest'dy and I finds 'em here on your doorstep.'

Joe, puzzled, pulls in his head and calls out: 'Lucy, come thi ways here a minute!'

Lucy comes and the pair of them bend over the rose bowl, expressing their wonder as to who could have presented them with such a lovely bowl of roses.

But Tom was not to be hoodwinked and, ordering them not to run away, a most unlikely proceeding for two elderly people not yet fully dressed, he went in search of Frank Smith. He soon returned accompanied by Frank, and there ensued a new version of the Battle of the Roses, in abridged form, as they argued over possession, who had stolen them and who had finally deposited them on the shop doorstep.

Meantime Miss Harriet was busy with her morning chores, blissfully oblivious of the stir she had caused.

Tom was most aggressive about the matter, and protested that Joe Stubbs be sent for, for he was certain he was the culprit, failing Joe and Lucy Wrigley who had been found in possession of the stolen property. With difficulty Frank Smith held his

G

sturdy henchman back from carrying out his threat, pointing out
that they had no proof of who was the culprit and that the wisest
course was to let the matter rest.

Frank, reading in the weekly paper a report of the Kingsmill
Flower Show, smiled at one item, 'The best bouquet of roses,
First Prize, J. Stubbs', and hoped his part-time gardener would
not read the newspaper report.

The most keenly awaited event in agricultural circles was the
Nettleworth Horse and Foal Show, held in Magna Park on the
August Bank Holiday Monday. There were always some good
entries from the Parva farms, but this year the stock on show
seemed better than ever. George Western's mare Ruby had borne
a splendid colt foal with good knees and hocks, and wide-chested
and dark brown like its dam, which looked a prize winner.
Ralph was showing in the class for the best matched plough team,
with two perfectly matched dappled greys out of Flower, the
grey mare. Farmer Robinson was again there with his hunter
mare Vashti with foal at foot.

In the show field on the auspicious day stood a long line of
horses of all breeds in their canvas stalls, excitement in the flash
of their eyes at the unaccustomed noise and bustle, and the music
of the band engaged to brighten up the proceedings. First in the
line came the Hunter Class, some with their foals, some waiting
to be ridden in their entry class. Then the Hackneys, those proud
conceited animals that came somewhere between the pony and
the cart-horse. Their watchword was 'action', and they stepped
around the ring showing their paces, drawing a queer four-
wheeled contraption, known as a 'sulky', of no material benefit,
except to be drawn around a show ring. The largest entries were
in the Shire Class, for in spite of the internal combustion engine
and the steam-driven truck the draught horse was still the
country's main motive power.

Horse dealers, wearing stiff, uncomfortable, starched collars,
and even stiffer and more uncomfortable breeches and gaiters of
white whipcord, hovered around the three- and four-year-olds,

hoping to bring about a sale for some prospective customer, who would condemn the proud colt to doing a daily round of the city streets until its feet became ruined with treading the granite setts—never more would it stand on its hind legs to give battle with its forefront as in its pride and glory of this present after-noon. Parva brought home its share of the honours. George Western's mare Ruby, with foal at foot, was judged the best mare with foal in the field, while Ralph, with his pair of greys, easily outpaced all other entries. Robinson's Vashti again came first for mares in the Hunter Class with foal at foot.

Another interesting class was for the best-groomed cart-horse. One felt sorry for the entrant that didn't get a prize, for groom-ing a cart-horse, and cleaning the harness to pass judgment under the scrutiny of the judge, takes weeks of toil and labour. Every buckle and strap is tested as to its ease or difficulty in being unfastened, every chink and crease in the leather is searched for a speck of dust, and finally the horse's harness is taken off while with a silk handkerchief the judge calmly wipes the horse's flank to see if perchance a speck of dust adheres to the silk. After which the carter may reclothe his steed in all its finery—brasses, bells, martingales, hip-straps and all its bravery of rosettes and caddis—while within his heart is a sinking feeling that he hasn't quite brought it off.

The tradesman's turn-out is not quite so exactingly scrutinized. The action of the horse is taken into account, perhaps even more than the originality and suitability of the vehicle to the particular tradesman, but be it butcher, baker or candlestick maker, the tradesman's turn-out makes a colourful event in the afternoon's performance.

There were pony races, there was 'Tilting at the Ring', with hunters and hacks, there was a large beer booth and a small tent where one could get tea or lemonade, and moreover there was a prize brass band playing overtures and serenades until dusk of evening, so that he must have been a sour-bellied curmudgeon who said he hadn't had his shilling's worth, which was the price of entry at the gate.

At 4 p.m. the competitors were allowed to take their chargers out of the show ground, and a happy cavalcade might have been seen descending Magna hill, bringing home the honours.

It was a warm evening of golden sunshine, and the hut and the Green were forsaken, for most of the young folk were up at Magna finishing off show day by riding on the dobby horses and the swings, whose steam organ had been blaring out 'Yip-i-addy-I-ay ever since mid morning. George Western, Frank Smith and Jon Keppel were reclining at ease in the shade of the hut discussing the affairs of the day. There was not a cloud in the sky and the only movable object on the horizon was a boy on a bicycle careering wildly down Magna hill with his feet on the foot rests.

'Yon youth'll break his flipping neck,' commented George, adding: 'And that'll leave more bread for them 'ats in need.'

No one heeded George's laconic statement and the boy, then entering the village, reared his bike on the causeway edge and lustily bawled out: 'England declares war on Germany! Special edition! England declares war on Germany!'

The storm had broken. 4th August 1914.

CHAPTER ELEVEN

For King and Country

WE WERE not greatly disturbed by the threat of war, for the Boer War in South Africa, which had failed to alter the placid routine of everyday life in Nettleworth Parva, was still fresh in our minds. Besides, did not Britannia still rule the waves, and was not ours the empire on which the sun never sets? Only Jonathan Keppel was more cautious in his outlook and warned us of the growing strength of Germany, and how only last year she had entered the mouth of the Thames with one of her dreadnoughts flaunting the banner 'Britannia no longer rules the waves'.

We tried to restore Jon's confidence by pointing out how Victoria the Good and Wise had wedded her offspring to most of the crowned heads in Europe, including the Kaiser, thereby insuring a close and lasting relationship wherein a major European war was most improbable. Our complacency was rudely shaken when, by September, several battalions of new recruits were encamped in the mill fields. Even so the war was not as yet taken seriously, not even by the happy, carefree recruits who paraded our one street, filled our hut for reading and lectures, and ogled the girls along the lanes and footpaths. Poor young lads in the golden sunshine, with as yet no inkling of the horrors to come, or of the uncertainty of ever seeing the green fields of England again once they had left its shores.

At the same time our village became denuded of its youth, who hurriedly responded to the call to arms lest the war should be ended before they had a chance to fire a shot. There was much discussion among the young fellows in the hut as to which regiment they should honour with their presence, with a distinct partiality for famous Scottish brigades, such as the Black Watch, the Seaforth Highlanders and the Scots Greys. They strode bravely to the recruiting office and were enlisted to serve in no less famous regiments: the Notts and Derby, the Green Howards or K.O.Y.L.I.s. The hut was saved from closing down for the 'duration' by the noble band of women, eternally sewing, knitting and packing food parcels for the troops, so that it became more busily engaged than ever. The troops, under canvas during that first war-time September, gradually melted away as more army huts and barracks were established in the country, and Parva felt more isolated than ever with the departure of its visitors along with its native youth. Perhaps our greatest loss was the Rev. Gilbert Malham, who soon after the outbreak of war became an army chaplain somewhere in France.

At the very outbreak of the war there was a rumpus at The Cedars. Miss Julia declared her intention of doing war work, much to Mama's horror, who tried to revive her former project of marrying her daughter off to the solicitor Percy and thus settling down secure from war's alarms. Julia resolutely refused, and repeated her determination to wed that horrid boy of Billy Brunt's. The outraged lady appealed to Miss Turbafield, her companion help, to instil reason into the headstrong Julia. Miss Turbafield mishandled her task by pointing out that many young ladies were now taking up work of some kind, and 'as for that boy of Brunt's, it was not for her to advise on so delicate a matter, but if they sincerely loved each other, then difference in status should be no bar to their becoming man and wife'.

Mrs Keppel's reply to this was to tell her companion help to find work of national importance instead of idling away her time at The Cedars, and accused her of having caused a breach between Miss Julia and her mother. Miss Turbafield packed her trunk and departed. Miss Julia, seeing departures very much in evidence, gathered together a few necessary belongings and left the very next day along with her old governess. Where they have gone no one knows for certain, but Miss Turbafield's home being in Birmingham, it is supposed that Birmingham was their destination. One feels sorry that this distress should have come to Mrs Keppel, for her character has completely altered for the better of late years. Friendly and considerate, for she has taken a leading part in the activities of the hut, it might be feared that the break with Julia would cause her to revert to her former proud and arrogant way of life. But misfortunes never come singly and Bessie the maid, on her next monthly pay day, gave in her notice, saying she was 'going on munitions'.

'Some go up and some go down', as the saying goes, and now Mrs Keppel does her own housework, assisted by Jubby the groom and gardener, and Mrs Stubbs the washerwoman, who comes two days per week instead of the former mere one.

Jubby has certainly gone up a grade, for whereas before he was not allowed over the doorstep on account of his filthy habits, he now enters the scullery as odd-job man, cleaning boots, knives, forks, spoons or doing any job that is too rough for the mistress's delicate hands. And they get on famously together.

It is now impossible to engage a maid or domestic help of any kind. All the womenfolk are making shell-cases in town or have joined in the war effort as land workers or in one of the many women's auxiliary services, and the seriousness of the situation is now forced upon us even in Nettleworth Parva and has awakened in us a determination to beat the Hun at all cost. The cost is great in agriculture, as in all walks of life. Farmer Western was justifiably proud of his stable of horses, of which there was none finer in the district. It had long been his custom to breed a couple of foals each spring, to be eventually broken in to trace work, then to shaft work. As four-year-olds the colts were sold for town work, where good limbs and sound feet are needed on the granite setts of city streets. The Army now began to commandeer the farm horses without so much as by your leave; and eventually the local vet, along with a horse dealer, called on George Western at Wheatlands Farm and took away four of George's best colts, leaving only a pair of ageing brood mares and an ancient trap-horse whose working days were supposed to be over. George was not addicted to strong language, but those two fellows who took away his best horses no doubt thought him quite adept at forceful self-expression. Still, it was upsetting to find one's horse power reduced to half strength, while the Government were pleading for increased production. They served all the farmers in the same abrupt way, and great concern was felt on how to sow and gather in the coming year's crops. It was here that Val Keppel came into prominence. George Western bought a tractor to help along until another pair of colts could be broken into harness during the following spring. Val, being more mechanically minded than Ralph, who had been brought up to horses, was given the office of tractor driver. A good job he made of it, too, getting the fields ploughed in less time than three pairs of horses would have needed to do the job.

Billy Brunt at this time, in a burst of patriotic fervour, decided to take up regular and honest labour for the good of the country, on the understanding that it was to be for the duration only. Frank Smith, too old to fight, joined the staff and became Billy's working companion at the many jobs that span the farming year. With the help of female labour they carried on gamely, and scarcely missed the powerful shire horses, without which successful agriculture was supposed to be impossible.

Ralph was periodically called up for examination by the Army Board and released to be called up later. By 1917 the position on the battle fronts became so serious that Ralph was conscripted to join up without further delay. This caused some resentment on the part of Ralph, who supposed that the first to go should have been Val, who was some years younger, besides being a war-time addition to the regular staff. The Board had looked on the matter in a different light. Val Keppel was the tractor driver, and to their idea the leading man on the farm, whereas Ralph now took only second place. It was a pity, really, for Ralph was a first-rate hand at any job on the farm, but there was nothing could be done about it, though the Westerns tried their utmost, for Ralph was looked upon as one of the family, having lived and worked on that same farm since leaving school at the age of thirteen. So they lost Ralph and Val reigned in his stead as the leading man on the farm.

A war-time measure was the creation of the Women's Land Army, and a very useful contribution they made towards the war effort. As a body they were smart, and efficient too, in their khaki breeches, leggings, smock and wide-brimmed hat. Some were put to dairying, some worked in the fields, while some, the Forage Corps, went round with the government threshing machines. No glamour attached to these latter, for threshing corn is always a dusty, dirty occupation, and all honour is due to the young women who travelled around with the threshing gang during the long war years. An episode concerning George Western's farm is connected with the threshing machine. The Army had requisitioned a stack of oats, and in due course sent a machine and its complement of Land Army girls to thresh out the corn, bale the straw and leave everything in order for transportation on army lorries. Thus the farmer and his men took no hand in the matter, all the labour being performed by the army corps.

In due course the farmer received a cheque to the value of the oats and the straw, for which he was thankful, though he resented the manner in which the authorities came and demanded his oat stack, without the formality of asking, 'Do you mind?' or 'Have you a stack of oats to spare?'

It was in this frame of mind, feeling sore that he could not now dispose of the produce of his land in the way he thought fit, that some months later Farmer George came in about mid morning after seeing his men engaged in their various jobs. This was always an occasion for a cup of tea while he looked over his morning mail. He opened an official envelope bearing the initials 'O.H.M.S.', and frowned—he was always being pestered with official envelopes nowadays.

'Why, what's this?' he remarked, drawing out a folded cheque. 'Another cheque in payment for that stack of oats they paid me for last year? They must be potty!'

'A mistake, I expect,' replied his wife. 'A clerical error, as they say.'

'Well, that's their look-out,' replied George, examining the cheque.

'Nay, lad, we are all liable to mistakes at times, and it can be sent back by tonight's post.'

'Can be, but will it? The way they push us about, requisition-
ing this and that as though the place belonged to 'em, it'll serve
'em reet if I get my own back on 'em.'

'George, thou shouldn't talk like that.'

'I'm sick to death o' the blooming war.'

'So is everybody, lad, and with more cause than we have.
Farmers are now better off than ever they were in peace time
and, George lad, we've been together on this farm nigh on
thirty years, first along with your dad, then later on our own,
and never once in all those years have I known you take what was
not your own.'

'You're reet, lass,' conceded George. 'I don't know what
came ower me to think o' such a thing, but you'd always more
sense in your little finger than I had in my yed.'

'Nay, lad, I won't have that. I've known when times were bad
and it was difficult to make ends meet for ourselves, when you've
gone out of your way to help a neighbour who was down on his
luck. It's just this horrid war, love—it plays havoc with people's
nerves, and they do things they wouldn't dream of doing in the
ordinary way of life.'

'Aye, Mabel lass, reet's reet,' remarked George, replacing
the cheque in the envelope. 'Thou's been worth thy weight in
gold to me, and but for thee I might ha' soiled my fingers wi' bad
money long ago.'

'Nonsense, love. Here, give me that envelope—there's Mary
coming across from the cattle sheds and we must not let her
know what evil nonsense we have been concocting.' Mabel,
otherwise Mrs Western, hastily thrust the envelope behind the
mirror on the mantelshelf.

Mary entered the living-room, wearing a pair of long trousers,
quite a startling and, as some people declared, unbecoming
innovation for the female sex; but trousers for women came to
stay, be they termed trousers, trews, slacks or what you will,
along with even more startling attire for the female figure.

'Anything interesting in the post, Mum?' inquired Mary,
pouring herself a cup of tea.

'There's a letter from our Lillian. She says it's very doubtful if she can get leave to come home for the wedding, as she's volunteered to go to France. I feel worried about our Lillian. I didn't mind her joining the V.A.D.s, as she'd set her mind on it, but I don't like the thought of her being abroad on hospital work in these evil times. But here's the letter—read it yourself, for she's written it for all of us.'

'It's a pity if she won't be here for my wedding. I was hoping to have her as a bridesmaid,' remarked Mary, after reading her sister's letter. 'But I will say this for our Lillian, she's got more guts than me. I should topple over at some of the things she has told me she has to do.'

'Thou'll topple ower all reet afore long,' remarked Dad facetiously, at which Mum frowned at him severely, so he changed his approach by saying: 'Why not postpone the wedding until after the war, then we can have a slap-up do with everybody here, and plenty to eat and drink on board, and none o' these damned coupons to bother about.'

'Don't take any notice of him, love, he's that way out this morning,' advised Mum, at which Mary crossed over to where Dad sat in his armchair and, ruffling his hair, or what remained of it, said: 'You are not cross, Daddy—not really, are you?'

'Well, I'm about the same, thank you, and how's yourself?'

'Fine, thanks, now I know you were only teasing, and you don't really want us to postpone our wedding. And now I must get back to the sheds, for the big white sow is close on farrowing, and she's such an ungainly creature, she will squash half of them out of existence if I am not there to rescue the little dears.'

Mary kissed the bald patch on the top of his head, then ran off to assist in the old sow's accouchement.

'Everybody works but Father, or so it seems,' chanted Dad, rising from his chair. 'I'll go and gi' 'em a hand wi' the mangolds while noon.'

A very happy wedding took place this summer in spite of war-time restrictions and the depressing news from the western front. In June Valentine Keppel and Mary Western were joined together in holy matrimony at the parish church of St Giles, our own little church not being licensed for weddings or funerals. Thus the two most important families have become united, and the happy couple now occupy part of the farmhouse at Wheatlands, which is commodious enough to hold them all without their treading on one another's heels. The reception was held in the hut at Mary's express wish, 'so that anyone can come who has a mind'. It appears that everyone did come, for the place was packed to the doors. It was a marvellous spread, considering how the country was so strictly rationed, both for food and drink. Old George was in fine feather for the occasion and scarcely recognizable in a light grey suit, with grey silk hat to match, though he had cut up rough the week before when Mary and her mother were discussing the wedding arrangements. They were deciding on which taxi proprietor to engage to convey the party to church, when George, in his bluff manner, remarked:

'What's amiss wi' a carriage and pair? A pair o' greys if it's possible to find such nowadays.'

'You are behind the times, Dad,' said Mrs Western. 'Everybody goes by taxi these days—weddings and funerals too.'

'Not me though,' retorted George; 'and if it's my funeral I'll be hoss-drawn or I'll get out and walk.'

'Don't be stupid, Dad; me and Mary can manage this affair without you butting in.'

'Oh, that's it, is it? Well, let me tell you this, I ain't giving my gal away to no man unless I can take her to church in a respectable carriage and pair.'

Mary, despairing of getting married at all owing to Dad's stubbornness, declared her willingness to be taken to church in one of the farm muck-carts if such was Dad's wish; and as for her own choice she preferred an open carriage to either a taxi or a muck-cart.

So on the auspicious day the bride and her attendants were conveyed up Magna hill in a carriage drawn by a pair of greys of no particular quality or breeding, but the best animals Farmer

George had been able to find after several days of intensive search of the countryside in his old Ford car. The invited guests who arrived at the church in various forms of transport considered that George had stolen a march on them as he gallantly helped his daughter out of an open carriage. To say the bride was lovely conveys but little meaning, for who ever saw a bride that was not lovely in her wedding dress? One can only say that Mary Western was of more than passing loveliness as she walked down the aisle on her father's arm. Her veil and long white train, secured by a chaplet of cream rose buds, half hid and half revealed the beauty of her gold-brown hair. Two small train-bearers, cousins to the bride, looked charming in cream-coloured tunics and white shoes and socks. As for the two brides-maids and all the gaily dressed females at the ceremony, what can a mere male do to describe them? His base and unworthy thought at the time was 'How many clothing coupons have been sacrificed to produce all this splendour?' It was difficult to make any lavish display even for a wedding owing to the rationing restrictions, but the recpetion in the hut seemed to lack for nothing. Of course the farmer was in an advantageous position compared with other people, especially those living in town. The Westerns, for instance, had a bacon chamber up in one of the garrets, which always held a year's supply of hams and flitches. It was an unthrifty housewife who cut into a ham or flitch before it had been hanging a twelvemonth to dry, so in that way they had always a year's supply in hand. There was very little shortage of milk, butter or eggs, the one vital scarcity being sugar of which the whole population was granted a very meagre ration.

But the feasting passed off merrily, with toasts, speeches and wisecracks, until it was time for the bridal couple to depart on their brief honeymoon in Matlock, at the invitation of Val's uncle, who resides in that charming place.

That Val and Mary were a well-liked couple was evidenced by the many lovely presents which had been set out for display on one of the tables. The question of whether it was wise or safe to have them so publicly exposed never entered anyone's head, though everyone in the village visited the place during the evening, when free drinks with cake and cheese were distributed to all comers. Ere the happy couple departed to catch a train towards Matlock George Western blatantly suggested that they postponed their honeymoon until 15th July as this fine open weather was sure to break on St Swithin's and they could disport themselves on High Tor in the rain when the hay was safely gathered in. Mary's only reply to this was a hug and a kiss, with a few tears of happiness shed on Dad's hefty shoulder while she calmed herself down sufficiently to bid the rest of the party farewell without a trace of emotion.

Even in Parva the war brought grief and distress, and the post girl would deliver at some cottage or other a fateful buff envelope informing some poor mother that her son had been killed in action. Young Peter Brunt, brother of Quiddy, a bright young fellow, was one of the first to be reported 'missing, assumed to have been killed', and the two sons of Charlie Butcher both fell in the battle of the Somme. The war, which we prophesied would be over by that first Christmas, continued to rage over Europe like a dragon spouting fire, until the most optimistic began to doubt if we should emerge victorious. It was Germany's ruthless method of warfare that eventually turned the tide in our favour with the sinking of the *Lusitania* in May 1915, with 1,198 passengers aboard. Of these 124 were American citizens and, though we did not realize it at the time, this action determined America's entry into the war. Even with her help victory was yet a long way off, and we seemed prone to disaster on sea and land. However, in spite of setbacks, we refused to give way to gloom and despair and kept the flag flying on the home front with numerous entertainments, along with efforts for the soldiers' comforts.

One thing for which we were grateful during the lean years of ration books was the opportunity of procuring a freshly killed rabbit, and even had Billy the poacher offered us a pheasant, conscience would not have protested.

But our main source of supply was Tushy the rat-catcher, who was eventually elevated by the county council to the title of pest officer. Tushy, past military age, became a war profiteer in a small way, in that he charged from two and six to three shillings for a rabbit which formerly he sold at ninepence or one shilling. The prices of all provisions rose to alarming heights, and until the Rent Restriction Act came into force house rents had risen in like proportion. This Act, though needful, brought great distress to certain elderly people, especially spinster ladies, who had been bequeathed a little property, perhaps a row of cottages which they let at a few shillings per week, seldom more than half a crown, to provide them with a modest income. They were now reduced to extreme poverty, and in some cases were unable to purchase the meagre ration allowed on their cards.

Though frequently called up for medical examination Joe Stubbs always returned home graded C 3, and we began to despair of Joe ever doing anything towards winning the war. Someone met him once returning from his periodical ordeal and inquired:

'How have you fared this time, Joe?'

'Why,' says Joe, 'I wer' watching a lot o' sojers stabbing bayonets into sandbags and I says to mi'sel, some'dy's going to get hurten doing like that if they're not careful, so I've decided to keep away from 'em, and I've come home.'

At length Joe was ordered to find work of national importance, but he was so long choosing a job suitable to his particular temperament that the powers that be attached him to a plate-laying gang on the railway, and Parva was rid of Joe until after the armistice; this, be it added, to the great satisfaction of Mrs Joe Stubbs.

CHAPTER TWELVE

Armistice

LOOKING back on the war years it is as though a great gulf had been cut in the world's history, a wide abyss into which have been cast all those things we used to believe in and accepted as good and sacred. Likewise we must add that much that was bad and discreditable now lies buried in that gulf. We had almost begun to accept war as our natural way of life, so that it came as a shock of surprise to learn that the war was over on the eleventh hour of the eleventh day of the eleventh month of the year 1918. We were now a different race of people, living in a different world, and even the returned Army have renounced the old order which, they said, gave us this devastating war. A war to end wars, they said, and spoke of a new world in which war and distress will have no part. We all hope this will be so, but with so much bitterness and hatred aroused during these last four years it will be difficult to avoid further bloodshed. Yet hatred is not the primal cause of war, for how can one hate the thing unknown and unseen? Hatred is not inborn in Nature which is ruled by fear, fear of the unknown and the law of self-preservation. Neither does the animal kingdom know anything of Love, a divine quality given only to the human animal who was made in God's own image. Even the mother sheep, given a strange lamb to rear, will hastily butt the little stranger aside, having no love for other than her own flesh and blood. So with all animals, the law of self-preservation causes them to drive away or kill the stranger and any of their number afflicted with disease or fallen by the wayside.

The human animal, imbued by his Creator with the spirit of Love, does none of these things, but nurses his sick, builds hospitals and takes the utmost care of his aged and infirm. Then, because he too is a child of Nature and subject to fear, he

destroys not his sick and infirm but the healthiest and fittest of his
young manhood under the law of self-preservation. This fear,
which engenders hatred, will ever fill the world with war and
distress, until perfect love has cast out fear.

We older people look back with longing on those quiet and
happy days on the other side of the gulf, though the younger
generation deride our simple ways and talk loudly of progress
and a land fit for heroes to live in. In spite of its poverty it had
much to recommend it, with tobacco at threepence per ounce or,
if one cared to indulge in the more expensive brands, fourpence.
It was customary, when the farmer's man took a load of grain to
town for him to be given one shilling as 'allowance money', and
with this splendid tip he could treat himself to half a gallon of
beer (10d), half an ounce of tobacco (1½d) and still have a
halfpenny in change. Beef and bacon were at from fourpence to
sixpence a pound, flour at tenpence a stone and a dozen boxes of
matches sold for twopence ha'penny. A pair of new boots cost
from six to eight shillings and a new cloth cap sixpence. Eggs at
their dearest were one penny each and butter never soared higher
than one shilling a pound.

Truly the farmer suffered greatly from these low prices, and
not until the appointment of a food controller in 1916 did
agriculture come on a sound footing, with subsidies on wheat,
whereby the housewife was able to buy a four-pound loaf for
ninepence without any loss to the farmer. The first food to be
rationed was sugar, of which there was a national shortage throughout the war. This has proved a permanent blessing to agriculture
in that it started the sugar-beet industry, which is now one of
its most profitable crops. Formerly we looked to Germany and
France for beet-sugar supply, and this being stopped during the
war we had to rely on cane-sugar from the West Indies. While
this gave a boost to the sugar-cane plantations the U-boat menace
caused the Board of Agriculture to foster home-grown beet sugar,
and they erected several processing plants in various parts of the
country, notably the beet factory at Kelham in 1918. Turnip
growing, which had been the basic root crop for sheep and

H

cattle, now gave place to marrow-stemmed kale, which proved a more nutritious and less expensive crop to grow than the swede turnip which had held sway from the days of 'Turnip Townshend' of the eighteenth century.

To return to domestic affairs, we have had a wedding in the village between no less persons than Ralph, the late ploughman at George Western's, and Bessie, the one-time maid at Mrs Keppel's. The Westerns were somewhat hurt at Ralph's behaviour after he was demobbed. His home is in the Trentside village of Beckford, and after leaving the Army he returned to his home village, as of course it was right and proper that he should first of all visit his parents. But the Westerns had expected him eventually to return to his former position on the farm, and Ralph knew it was being kept open for him. Therein he was remiss in cutting himself off entirely from his old place where he had been treated as one of the family for so many years. During his army service Mabel Western had never missed sending him a food parcel containing tobacco and other tokens of her regard, and she felt it much that she should be so ignored. One can only assume that Ralph was resentful at having been called up for active service, while Val Keppel, a newcomer, had been granted exemption. Ralph was known to have visited Parva on several occasions to keep up his attachment with Bessie, whose home is in the village, yet not once did he call on the Westerns to thank them for their kindness. As for Bessie, little had been seen of her after she left The Cedars to work on munitions, but doubtless she remained the bright and cheerful young lady who attended the hut meetings occasionally.

Compared with Val and Mary's wedding theirs was not a sumptuous affair, though it was known that Bessie had been a regular investor in Government War Loan. The reception was held at the King's Head in Magna and about twenty friends and relatives were present. Perhaps it is unfair to make comparisons, but the affair did not seem to go off with the swing and careless rapture that had marked the nuptials of Val and Mary. They were not of course quite on the same social level, and where Val and his bride were but in their twenties Ralph and Bessie had reached their thirties. But even so Bessie looked pale and wan, her features drawn, and not a bit like the Bessie who was the maid at The Cedars and whose healthy oval cheeks bore a perpetual smile. The gentleman of the party put the alteration down to the stress of the war years, though some of the ladies put forward a more sinister reason. The wedding took place one October week-end, and Ralph took his bride home to his parents' house in Beckford for a short honeymoon until the following Tuesday, when they took up their abode with Bessie's parents until a suitable house could be found. Ralph still showed no desire to return to the farm, but found work on a road-widening scheme that was taking place on Magna hill. Alas for the charm of our little village, plans have been put forward whereby Parva is to be absorbed into Nettleworth Magna. Sewage and water mains are being laid between the two places, and houses, of the bungalow type, are already being erected on Magna hill. They say that Parva is now a development area, whatever that may mean, and it seems as though Parva as a quiet little backwater where nothing ever happens is finished.

The serious influenza epidemic towards the close of the war had no alarming effect on our healthy locality, though it claimed two victims who were greatly missed. The most prominent of the two was Mrs Keppel, who was looked upon with some esteem in the neighbourhood owing to her many social activities, her latest act of grace being acceptance of the presidency of the recently formed branch of the Women's Institute. It was pleasing to note that her daughter Julia managed to come to the funeral, her first visit home since her quarrel with her mother. Evidently the quarrel between mother and daughter was more serious than one imagined, seeing that it kept them apart until it was too late to make amends. She had, so it appears, kept in touch with her brother Val, who says she got married the year after the war ended. Who her husband was even he was not told, except that she had married the man of her choice.

The other victim of the epidemic was our old friend Billy Brunt the poacher, but as always with Billy there was a shadow of doubt about the case. He had now reached the honourable and pensionable age of seventy years, which coincided with the Government having raised the rate of pension from seven and sixpence to ten shillings per week. Billy considered this as worthy of some celebration, for he was always one for celebrations, was Billy. He duly drew his pension at Magna post office, after which he called at the Red Lion along with a few friends. He seems to have visited various other houses of refreshment during the day, after which the hour of his return home is unknown. A policeman found him lying unconscious by the roadside near the new building site on Magna hill, around the hour of midnight. Billy was taken by ambulance to the hospital, where he expired a few days later from, so it was said, influenza. They are charitably minded people at Nettleworth Parva.

We have lost our curate, the Rev. Gilbert Malham, though happily he is still alive. He stayed one year in his old curacy at Magna, when we feted his home-coming, looking forward to his revival as producer of plays in the hut, but he has now accepted the living of a vicariate in the diocese of Southwell in Nottinghamshire, to which he takes our best wishes for his future welfare.

Though we greatly missed the Rev. Gilbert's lead in the activities of the hut, we overcame the loss by the aid of one of the families who had erected objectionable red-brick bungalows that were bound to spoil the look of our village. Mrs Knowles has studied dramatic art and has proved herself a competent producer, many people claiming her to be better than the curate, but for my part I favour the Rev. Gilbert with his wit and neat turn of words and phrases. However, the hut is now flourishing again in all its pre-war activities, and though some of the old leaders have had to yield office to younger hands owing to old age and infirmity, these younger leaders are as capable, I am sure, and as enterprising as were the old pioneers, who by trying to preserve the amenities of our obscure little village have placed it on the map.

Change is in the air, even in Nettleworth Parva, and a surprising change is that George Western has retired from farming and turned the farm over to his son-in-law Val and to his daughter Mary. Or supposedly so, for the old fellow contentiously finds fault with Val's method of management, declaring that the farm is going to ruin, that he is bleeding the land to death and that in a few years' time it will grow nothing. Fortunately neither Val nor Mary take any notice of Dad's despotism, but accept his criticisms in the best of good humour. Val follows the new trend in farm practice, concentrating on such crops as sugar-beet, potatoes and kale. Sugar-beet and potatoes, by the way, are sold off the land, and thus return no humus to the soil in the form of animal manure, whereas under the old 'four-course system' practised by George the root crop was always swedes or turnips, to be eaten off by the sheep and cattle, thus returning humus and fertility to the soil. This method had never varied through several generations of agricultural practice. The first year fallow, when the soil was liberally dressed with manure and fertilizer for the root crop. The following year the field was sown with barley, the most profitable of the corn crops, being in great demand for malting by the breweries. While the barley crop was growing it was undersown with 'small seeds', that is clover and rye-grass. Thus the third year the field was down to clover, either red for mowing or white for sheep pasture. The field that carried a flock of sheep during the summer would get a good dressing of sheep dung and so was usually sown with wheat for the fourth-year crop, whilst the other field, which would be partially grazed after the hay crop was gathered, would bear a crop of oats. It was a sound and worthwhile system, and one can see old George's point of view in the matter and his dismay at seeing the produce carted away instead of being returned to the soil. In Val's favour it must be said he was making a greater profit per acre than ever his father-in-law achieved, and for his sheep he grows kale as requiring less expense in labour.

Where Farmer George kept a herd of twelve dairy cows Val has now a herd of twenty-four and has forsaken the old Shorthorn

breed for a black and white breed introduced from Holland.
They are lovely animals, known as Dutch or British Friesians.
Val is cautious and business-like in his methods, and has gradually
built up his herd over the years by replacing the Shorthorns
with young Friesian stock. Only occasionally has he bought an
imported Dutch Friesian, and old George has not been informed
of the price paid for these animals or the fireworks would go up
indeed. Nowadays, I am afraid, old George is treated with a
lovable contempt. Most of George's despotism is just pretence,
for in reality he is very proud of his son-in-law's go-ahead
methods and never tires of proclaiming his prowess to anyone
outside the family circle. There is one member of the farm with
whom George never finds fault, that is young George Valentine
Keppel, aged three and a half, who bids fair to become spoilt by
his indulgent grandsire. Mary affirms that never when she was a
child dared she take such liberties with her dad as does that young
rogue.

They are indeed a happy family at Wheatlands Farm, and
George's wife Mabel, with scarce a grey hair on her head, looks
as spritely and bonnie as ever. Their younger daughter Lillian,
who took up hospital work during the war in the Voluntary Aid
Detachment, later to be known as the V.A.D.s, has now entered
the nursing profession as a career. A noble calling, so hard-
worked and so under-paid.

Spring is here, and the farmers are busy sowing their corn.
The rooks are busy in the corner of the wood, repairing their
last year's nests and making incessant clamour over the business.
They are wily birds, those rooks, for not a sound do they make
as they float down in a dense black cloud to feast on the new-
sown corn. Only a solitary rook remains as sentinel in the tree
tops where, on the approach of man, he gives a warning 'croak'
and up rises the black mass on the instant, to start again their
noisy din in the tree tops. Certain misguided damsels at the
commencement of the late war had a flair for issuing a white
feather to any poor youth not in khaki. At this present time the

slogan is, 'What did you do in the Great War?' I pass the
question on to my woodland friends, the rooks; the badger, now
spring-cleaning her sett; the fox, with her nursery in the covert;
and all those denizens whose way of life is to live dangerously.
'What did you do in the Great War?' How fortunate are these
creatures of a lower order who followed the usual routine of
Nature, knowing nothing of mass destruction, ration books or the
cold hand of D.O.R.A.

The low-lying mill fields are now yellowed over with butter-
cups and the higher pastures white with daisies, as though war
and distress had never been, and all the world looks bright and
gay. On Edward Robinson's farm the horseman was drilling
barley, and a youth was covering in the seed with the light
harrows. The youth is one of Tushy the rat-catcher's sons, who
started work for Mr Robinson when he left school at the
beginning of the war. He seems to have taken to farm work,
which is a good thing, for many of the rising generation have gone
on the new building sites where the pay is greater and the hours
are less. Still, the farm worker's wage is not too bad nowadays,
the Agricultural Wages Board having fixed a minimum of
twenty-five shillings for a fifty-hour week, which is an improve-
ment on the pre-war seventeen shillings. A pleasing thing about
the youth, Bert Whysall, is that he is intensely horse proud, and
today, with the sun shining on the horses' well-groomed skins
and reflecting the brilliance of their polished face-brasses, it
looks as if Bert has the making of a first-class horseman. The pair
he was driving were a red-roan in colour, perfectly matched, a
mother, and her four-year-old filly. It was a treat to watch them
pounding the earth as though purposely keeping in step. There
are two shades of colour in roans, the red-roan which carries a
thick golden mane, and the blue-roan of a more sombre hue,
with a silvery-black mane, usually thin and coarse.

I hear that Ralph Cottom and his wife have settled down to
married life on The Brecks. This is a piece of waste land on the
edge of the village as one goes on the way to Far Commons of

about two acres in extent, much of which is bare rock and jutting crag. They took over last autumn, bought a caravan to dwell in and intend to try their luck as market gardeners. I am gravely concerned that Ralph's enterprise may fail, for it seems impossible for anyone to wrest a living from that stony waste. However one views Ralph's behaviour since his return from the war, it is sad to think of his sinking his war gratuity and any savings Bessie may have stored away in so doubtful a venture. I feel more hopeful after visiting The Brecks. Bessie greeted me over the top half of the caravan door, but kept herself hidden from view, which I thought strange, for Bessie was usually a chatty person and never averse to passing the time of day.

'You will find Ralph down in the sheds,' she remarked, and turned indoors to her work.

I found the sheds down the field. What had formerly been a derelict stone-built barn and an eyesore to anyone walking to the common Ralph had repaired and converted into weatherproof piggeries and poultry houses. After a hearty handshake and saying how pleased he was to have me call on him Ralph showed me round his stock. It was amazing what he had done in so short a time.

'Them'll be ready for the butcher next week,' he remarked, pointing to where seven thriving porkers were snoring in somnolent comfort on their straw bed. In another pen a large white sow lay suckling nine little piglets. Indicating the spacious interior of the barn, he explained how he hoped to expand with his pig breeding and the feeding of porkers for the butcher.

'But we have to go steady at first,' he explained. 'Learn to walk before we attempt to run, eh? Things are a bit tight at present, for most of the brass we had saved is laid out in stock, and when we draw for these porkers it'll be the first return we've had, except for the sale of a few eggs each week.'

'And what about your job on the council's road-widening scheme?'

'Finished last week, sir—Bessie's near her time. I shall miss Bessie until she gets on her feet again. She saw to things while I was at work. Been a wonderful help she has and dug up most of half an acre of this waste during the winter.'

'Is Bessie not well then?' I asked, not quite sure what Ralph was driving at.

'I expect having to fetch the fire engine any time now,' replied Ralph, still speaking enigmatically. They were wed in October, and it was as yet only mid April.

I stayed to have a word with Frank Smith and his wife. Frank is showing signs of his age, and is no longer the dapper little figure of former years. He seldom gets out and about these days owing to rheumatism, brought on probably by living in the damp, insanitary cottage he bought so gleefully when he first came to dwell in Parva. Nevertheless he was an active and diligent 'special' during the war, most assiduous in seeing that no glimmer of light penetrated our blacked-out windows. Gone are those splendidly waxed moustachios in which he took such pride, and all one sees on his upper lip are a few straggly grey hairs which betoken him a true born countryman. He still shows great interest in his adopted village, and when I mentioned to him of my visit to Ralph's he seemed greatly concerned, saying that he too must pay him a visit. The 'fire engine', in the form of the village midwife, called at The Brecks two days later and delivered Bessie of a baby daughter. Frank called to give his congratulations, and found the caravan under new management, Bessie's mother, Mrs Meeke having taken over until such time as her daughter was able to get about again. Mrs Meeke is a well-conducted sort of person, modest and with none of that loose talk which is so prevalent with some of the cottage wives, and a respected member of the hut sewing party and of the Women's Institute. After viewing Bessie and her baby lying in bed, which he found somewhat of an ordeal, and saying a few words suitable to the occasion, Frank descended the caravan steps with the intention of having a word with Ralph, busily engaged on his holding. Mrs Meeke followed him outside and, folding her arms inside her white apron, remarked: 'Well, I'm glad she's getten it over.'

'Yes,' replied Frank, not knowing what else to say.

'Of course it's come afore its time, as the first one often does.'

'Er—yes,' was again the reply.

'I'm glad as things has worked out all right.'

'Er—yes, I suppose so, Mrs Meeke.'

'I will say this of our Bessie, she ain't a bad girl, never was. Brought up good and proper, and then to be caught like this!'

'Yes, I remember her as the maid at Mrs Keppel's, very modest.'

'Eh, dearie me,' went on Mrs Meeke, winding her arms more tightly inside her apron. 'I could see this lot coming about when Ralph started staying the week-end at our house.'

'I suppose you could have forbid his staying, Mrs Meeke?'

'It wouldn't ha' been no use, mister, if they're that way given; if they cannot roll over i' bed, they'll roll over i' the hedge bottom, and it's a sight more comfortable a-tween the sheets. Ralph's a good husband and thinks the world o' our Bessie. We are as God made us and the only sin is in being found out; it's easy enough to start a fire, but it ain't always so easy to bate it if it gets a-gait, and so after that first time I used to lie a-listening for the floorboards creaking, hoping the wedding would come afore the wailing.'

In spite of the stern disapproval of Mr Smith, or the easy acceptance of Mrs Meeke, Bessie was soon out and about again, and the Cottoms at The Brecks flourished wonderfully well. Within the space of a few years the Cottoms became the talking point of the village, for whatever their failings in some respects they were a pair of workers. They have increased their vegetable ground to more than an acre in extent, for though the soil was supposed to be thin and bare, most of their area proved to be a rich deep loam. They have now planted twenty young apple trees along with several rows of soft fruit, mostly raspberries and currant bushes. Ralph has acquired a plough and a pair of army-surplus horses, which though not of the shire breed, beloved of George Western, are useful animals. As for pigs and poultry, one wonders how two pair of hands can cope with all the work. Added to this they have a thriving business hawking vegetables from door to door every Friday in Nettleworth Magna, while in between whiles Bessie has produced three infants, two girls and one boy, in the space of four years.

Last Sunday afternoon the Cottoms were invited to tea at the Smiths' cottage, mainly at Mrs Smith's request, for Frank is rather shocked at Bessie's rapid production of babies, which, he thinks, borders on the vulgar. Indeed he has been known to remark that Bessie will eventually develop into a Mrs Brunt, crooning her youngest born among a pile of soiled nappies. Mrs Smith, on the other hand, never having been blessed with offspring of her own, has taken a great fancy to the infant Cottoms, and spends much time in making little garments on their behalf. Thus it was that they were invited to take tea in the front parlour at Clematis Cottage.

Frank Smith, never having done much in the way of entertaining infants, did very well for a novice. He got along famously with Elizabeth, aged three, and Ralph, aged two, by making a rabbit out of his pocket handkerchief. Mary, the youngest, being but one year of age, refused to be amused by his antics, nor was she impressed by any coo-ings or gurgles he produced for her benefit. It was when the party gathered round the table that Frank particularly noticed Bessie. He was most uncomfortably shocked, for Bessie has of late followed the modern trend of having her hair bobbed, instead of the decent 'bun' coiled at the nape of the neck. He felt most embarrassed and tried to look the other way, but somehow his eyes would revert back to look with disgust at Bessie's bared neck and shoulders. It was most unbecoming in the mother of three young children, and he made a mental note that never again must Bessie take tea in his house. He took another furtive glance and noticed that she wore a low-necked blouse, which exposed her plump shoulders and shapely arms, to say nothing of the top of her breasts, to the public gaze. It was indecent, to say the least, and to avoid further temptation to look that way he turned his attention on Ralph, who was at least decently attired, and together they discussed cabbage and other horticultural topics. What the two ladies were discussing he neither knew nor cared until his wife broke in to remark:

'Excuse me, Frank, did you hear what Bessie was saying?'

'No, I'm sorry,' replied Frank, turning his gaze in that direction and again noticing Bessie's pink and fleshy arms, with an almost irresistible desire now to give them a playful pinch.

'Has not Ralph told you? They are thinking of building themselves a house on The Brecks.'

'Thinking is about as far as we shall get, I'm afraid,' broke in Ralph. 'It's one of Bessie's ideas.'

'It's like this, Frank,' continued Mrs Smith. 'Bessie tells me they have not enough ready money as yet to lay out on a building project, and wondered about the advisability of approaching a money-lender at a fair rate of interest. I advised her to ask your opinion first before doing anything rash, as you understand these money matters.'

'Good gracious, no!' was Frank's reply. 'It would be a most risky business. Not that the money-lender would be dishonest, but he would demand a fair rate of interest on his loan, depending on how long you would be in repaying it. You seem to be doing fairly well at present, Ralph, but you cannot guarantee the future, and it would be a sad calamity if you had to sell your holding to pay off the mortgage.'

'That's my opinion, sir,' replied Ralph, who showed little enthusiasm for the project.

'My advice', continued Frank, turning to Bessie, 'is to stick to your caravan until you feel more financially secure.'

'But, Mr Smith, we can't wait,' declared Bessie, turning on him her most bewitching smile. 'We are already overcrowded with three babies, and there's no telling if it will stop at three lying alongside a great hefty fellow like our Ralph.'

'Just so, my dear,' replied Frank with a smile, though somewhat shocked at Bessie's outspoken way of putting it.

'Not that I mind a large family,' mused Bessie, 'but I must have somewhere to house the little dears.'

Here Mrs Smith interposed to say: 'I have been wondering, Frank dear, seeing that Ralph and Bessie are well known in the village as an honest and hard-working couple, if some private individual would be willing to help them with a loan.'

'It's an idea, anyhow,' mused Frank, 'and preferable to being tied to a money-lender.'

'Mr Smith,' broke in Ralph, 'the land agent has offered to sell me as much land as I need to build a house at ninepence a square yard. Have you any idea what the cost would be to build, say, a three-bedroomed house on around five hundred square yards of ground?'

'Why, I could not say offhand Ralph—prices are soaring these days—but I would guess a hundred and fifty pounds would cover everything.'

'Splendid!' exclaimed Bessie. 'I can see smoke going up our new chimney already.' Bessie rose from her chair, placed her youngest born on its father's knee and deliberately seated herself alongside Frank Smith. He recoiled in alarm and decided to be cautious on how he dealt with this product of the new age. Perhaps it was her nearness to him, perhaps it was the strong perfume of violets that pervaded her presence, or it may have been his being unused to the view of a woman's bared neck and shapely arms that overcame his prim and proper rectitude. A feeling of powerlessness came upon him.

'Mr Smith,' she purred, placing her shapely arm across the back of his chair, 'you have been so sweet and helpful already that it's a shame to trouble you further, but I wonder, could you give me any advice on how to set about this business of building a house—who we have to see and that kind of thing?'

Frank tried to regain some of his fast-ebbing dignity and remarked rather brusquely: 'Why, of course you must first of all secure a loan—a delicate business, I can assure you; even if you have friends with money to spare they may not be willing to hand out a hundred and fifty pounds without some security.'

Bessie pursed her lips, looked thoughtful, pressed her bare shoulder a little closer on Frank's shoulder and asked:

'What next?'

'Well, you must see an architect and surveyor—you will require a plan of the building—then a building contractor.' Frank paused, then added: 'What a pity my old gardener, Tom Pippin, is not still with us. He would have been the very man for the brick-laying—direct labour—it would have saved you pounds.'

'His son Tom is a bricklayer,' broke in Ralph. 'Me and Tom have been pals for years. He lives at Magna now and I see him most Fridays when I'm up that way. Guess he'd take the job on if I ask him, nights and week-ends, and mayhap o' Sundays.'

'And I will see an architect tomorrow,' declared Bessie, 'and, oh dear, isn't it frightening, some of the folk I shall have to see?' She gave Frank a mighty hug, saying: 'You are such a dear I could kiss you.'

Something quite out of keeping with Frank's staid and sober character came over him in consequence of Bessie's mighty hug. He actually patted her bared shoulder and said: 'There, there, my dear, do not worry your pretty head about architects and money-lenders. Leave everything to me. I know several of these people personally and will see to the whole business, arranging for the work to start as soon as possible.'

The Cottoms had to return home at six o'clock to attend to their stock and to put their babies to bed, and Frank sank into his chair, bewildered in the extreme. He recalled how on first seeing Bessie in her shorn locks and short skirts, he had resolved, within himself, that the perpetrator of so immodest an exhibition should never darken his doors again, and how, but a few minutes ago, he had shaken hands with that same exhibit, pressing her most earnestly to 'call again soon'. He bethought himself of Ulysses, tempted by the sweet music of the Sirens and groaned: 'Why, oh why, did I not, like Ulysses, steer myself clear?'

A more mortifying thought came to him. Was this a nefarious plot staged to wheedle him into helping the Cottoms financially and materially in the erection of their house? Ralph, he assured himself, was of too open and ingenuous a nature to be guilty of such subterfuge. An even more disturbing thought arose. Was his own wife, Elsie, a party to this trickery?

Frank Smith shuffled uneasily in his chair, and, perhaps for the first time in his career, uttered a vulgar and unqualified 'Damn!'

CHAPTER THIRTEEN

Brave New World

FOR good or ill our once charming little hamlet is fast disappearing under the march of progress. Sewage, gas and water mains have already reached Nettleworth Parva, while houses and bungalows now line both sides of Magna hill, so that Parva has lost its identity as a separate unit. In the Mill fields notice boards have sprung up advertising 'Building Plots for Sale', and many of the old stone cottages have been condemned as being insanitary. The quaint old shop, kept by Mrs Joe Wrigley, erstwhile Mrs Humble, has been enlarged and rebuilt in red brick, which so upset Mrs Joe that she retired, and, along with Joe, now lives in some trust cottages in Magna. It grieves one to see the place filling up with strangers, so that one seldom meets a soul whom one knows personally; even they, like oneself, are elderly and infirm. But it is all to the good, we are told, and we must move with the times which, they assert, will bring trade and prosperity into Parva. So it seems, for Parva is now so thriving a place that a Friday market is held on the Green. This began a few years ago with one solitary fish stall, and has now expanded so that some half-dozen stall-holders find it worth their while to display their goods for the delectation of our residents. I took a walk round one Friday evening and was quite impressed by the display.

I joined the edge of a crowd where a fellow with a bulbous-mottled nose of red and blue was selling cures for all the ills that flesh is heir to. Considering myself fairly sound I was horrified to learn that I was suffering from virulent forms of diseases of the liver, the lungs, the bladder and in fact of all the accessories from the scalp to the toe-nails. Heaven bless the man, for he—and he only—had the power to rescue me from the grave; doctors were useless, and he only had the formula that would save my life which he was willing to do at the small charge of one shilling per box. Strange how indifferent the crowd were to their 'length of days'. Here was a gentleman almost bursting his lungs on their behalf as he held aloft a small box, calling out 'One shilling only, ladies and gentlemen! One shilling!' until, finding that the crowd preferred death to his cures, he gradually lowered his price by inverse instalments from one shilling to threepence. I passed along in reflective mood, thankful that I had not bought a gold watch, nor a new ready to wear suit, for of what use to me would be these things seeing that I had refrained from buying a box of life-restoring pills?

Rather depressing, I found, were these stall-holders on the Green, and was pleased to come across the potman, whom I found to be much more interesting. He, however, does not hire a stall like our weekly visitors but draws his van up on the roadside and displays his wares on the grass. His periodical visits date back to time immemorial, and no one remembers the time when the first pot cart set up on the village Green. He wears a billycock hat of ancient lineage and has a loud voice and an extremely red face, due no doubt to his vociferous exertions in disposing of his wares. He owes nothing to the vendor of pills, for his lungs are as sound as brass. It fills one with wonder to see the potman manipulate a pile of plates as though they were a pack of cards, then spread them haphazardly on the grass without the least damage to one of them. His disparagers declare that his crockery are cast-outs from the pottery, and are misshapen or have a blemish of some kind, but what matter so long as the cups at one penny each hold their liquid and the platters hold their beef and veg without thrusting the gravy over the low side of the plate's circumference? Indeed the pot-seller is the most patronized of all our itinerent traders, for odd cups, saucers and plates are always in demand.

Occasionally, though only once in a while, a woman will push to the front of the crowd, and modestly whisper something in the potman's ear. He immediately climbs into his van, and presently emerges with something wrapped securely in stiff brown paper, so that no one may hazard a guess at the parcel's

I

contents. These whispered requests, I vouch, will become more rare as time goes on, for most of the new houses they are erecting have upstairs lavatories. We are certainly a thriving, go-ahead people compared with pre-war Parva, and the older residents, as they view the throng on the Green on market night, may be excused a sigh for the days gone by when they erected one solitary hut on the Green for the enlightenment of the village folk.

Another sign of progress is that we have our coal delivered by lorry. Our former coal dealer, Ben Travis, has passed away along with his lean and tired horse and his son Tom reigns in his stead. Tom Travis was one of the lucky few who went through the war without permanent injury, and with his war gratuity bought himself a one-ton Ford lorry to assist in his father's coal business. Whether the Ford is in every way superior to horse transport is a matter of individual opinion, but certainly the Ford never lies down with a load of coal on its back as did Ben's horses, though it has a habit of refusing to work for no apparent reason. On these occasions Tom will be seen laid on his back under the Ford's belly, performing some mysterious rite, after which, with a violent fit of shivering, a few minor explosions and a great deal of smoke from its exhaust, the lorry continues on its way. We are not yet so far advanced as to have a cinema in the village. But the enterprising Tom has bought a twelve-seater bus with which he transports the cinema patrons to and from the Globe at sixpence per head, or eightpence return. Young Tom should go far. The most popular picture showing at present seems to be *Tarzan of the Apes*, though a very dramatic picture of recent weeks was *The Four Horsemen of the Apocalypse*.

Of all the wonders of this new age the most remarkable is surely wireless telegraphy, which has quite outdated the gramophone as a source of entertainment. Frank Smith's gramophone recitals, once so popular, would attract very few customers today, even if the old gentleman were capable of following his former pursuits in the Community Hut. This wireless craze is spreading rapidly and nearly every house in the village is adorned with a wireless pole, so that from a distance the village has the appearance of a harbour with the masts of fishing vessels showing behind the houses. It seems quite unbelievable, but tonight we heard the Prince of Wales speaking at the opening of the British Empire Exhibition, and his voice was as distinct as though he were here in the room. The one snag about this remarkable discovery is the need for the earphones, of which our set has but two, so that only two persons can listen in at the same time. But it really was marvellous hearing His Royal Highness speaking all that distance away and is surely a reminder of how this new invention will knit far-away subjects nearer to the throne. What a fortunate kingdom is ours! With thrones toppling all over Europe the English monarchy stands firm in the affection of its people, with a well-loved King George V. Long may he reign, and a son to follow in the person of Prince Edward of Wales, than whom no heir to the throne has ever been more popular and who has won the esteem and affection of the whole world.

Last Sunday quite a party of us made the journey up to Magna for the unveiling of the Nettleworth War Memorial. What a sad occasion it is as one reads the long list of names of the fallen, four of them from the then small hamlet of Parva. Quite a crowd had gathered in the market-place to witness the ceremony, attended by member of the Urban District Council and other notabilities. The sculptor of this noble cenotaph, so I hear, was W. Brunt, which sets me wondering whether it could possibly have been 'Quiddy', who disappeared from our village so many years ago.

Customs and fashions may change, but Nature never alters her ways. I am reminded of this because it is now September, and the harvest is spoiling in the fields owing to the incessant rain. The weather broke on St Swithin's, 15th July, and no amount of 'poo-pooing' will alter the fact that it usually does. Some people are inclined to blame the wireless for the protracted spell of wet, though I read in the papers how Sir Oliver Lodge refutes the notion. For my part during my long acquaintance with harvests we have had more wet summers than dry ones before ever the wireless came into action, and it would be well to remember that it is the rain and clouds that make this country a green and pleasant land, that perpetual sunshine creates the desert and that a month of hot sunshine on our fields is as much as we can bear. Ralph and Bessie are comfortably settled in their new house, which for reasons of economy was built of red brick, so out of keeping with the wild beauty of The Brecks. They are thriving wonderfully, so much so that they have now a family of five. At long last we have got a public house in the village, which was opened last Saturday with free drinks all round. I hope I have not done injustice to the building by calling it a pub, or even an inn, for in flourishing letters of gold is inscribed the name, 'The Prince of Wales Hotel—Proprietor, E. Munday'.

The recent war has changed the pattern of our lives even more than at first we had realized. A recent house-warming party at The Cedars is a case in point, for it just could not have happened in the pre-war days. Our host was Jonathan Keppel, now grey-haired but active for all his seventy years. Next in order of merit was his son Val, along with the son's wife Mary Keppel. Mr and Mrs Frank Smith, though not of the family, were invited as old and particular friends. These few may be said to represent the high class or top dogs of the social world, for the other guests were plebeian indeed, and by birth or nature, or perhaps both, were undoubtedly underdogs, and not to be noticed in polite society, in the person of Mrs W. Brunt, relict of poacher Billy, and at present daily help at The Cedars, and John Jubb, alias 'Jubby', gardener and handy-man to Jon Keppel. Why it should be called a house-warming party is easily explained. The Cedars is now under entirely new management due to the home-coming of Julia and her husband William, more popularly known as Quiddy Brunt.

Julia was hostess for the occasion, a duty which she performed with all the dignity and grace which characterized her younger days; not quite the Julia whom we used to know, though with the same dark ringlets clustering round her neck and the same dark, flashing eyes that seem to suggest a fiery disposition if provoked. But that once haughty and overbearing manner has given place to a sweet amiability and a pleasant smile as she bids 'welcome' to her guests.

The most taciturn member of this pleasant gathering was Quiddy, who seems to have developed into a man of few words, though the fact of his walking with a limp and the aid of a walking-stick may be contributory factors to his manner having changed from that of a lively schoolboy. Nevertheless there was a special welcome from everyone for the returned Quiddy whom no one had seen or heard mention of for so many years.

Frank Smith had always been interested in the young Quiddy, and as they sat round the tea table, everyone asking questions of the two wanderers, he inquired: 'How about your career, Quiddy—still a monumental mason?'

'Still a mason, Mr Smith, monumental or otherwise,' replied Quiddy, 'though plaster and cement have ousted stone for sculptural work.'

'And about time too,' broke in Val; 'it seems ridiculous to me to be chipping away at hard granite when the same effect can be procured with plaster or cement.'

Quiddy pursed his lips, gave a thoughtful grin and replied: 'Not quite the same, Val. There's a world of difference between the mason's effort, cut out of the living stone, and something put together in a plaster mould. Almost anyone can work in plaster or cement, slapping a bit on here and scraping a bit off there, until he makes a perfect copy of his model. But with the stonemason the model lies hidden in the solid block of stone or granite, until with chisel and painstaking chips the sculptor reveals what he sees in the heart of the stone.'

'Hear, hear, Brunt,' broke in Jon Keppel. 'You know the great fault with our Val is, he's gone scientific and thinks the easiest way is always the best, even with his agricultural affairs!'

'Well, Dad, usually it is, and I see no point in making work into hard labour when their's an easier way of doing it.'

'So say they all these days,' grunted Jon Keppel.

Frank Smith returned to the subject of Quiddy's career and inquired: 'Why did you never write to us, Quiddy, and where have you been living this long while?'

'Well, sir, the last place I lived in was Exeter, though I was doing fairly well before the war on church fabric up and down the country, until I settled down in Exeter from choice. Julie being in Birmingham at that time, we never lost touch with each other, and we were in fact thinking of coming home and letting you know I had won through, when the war broke out and upset all my plans. I joined the Royal Marines at the outbreak of war, and eventually got damaged in a landing party in the Dardanelles. That ended my career as a soldier, for after spending a year in hospital being patched up I was honourably discharged as being of no further use as cannon fodder. I went back to my old lodging in Exeter, that being the address from which I had enlisted. They were grand people and welcomed me back as one of the family.'

'Dardanelles, eh,' mused Jon Keppel. 'That reminds me of old Jubby here. Do you remember? You used to pronounce the word as Jarganelles, Jubby lad.'

Jubby grinned and offered no reply, being somewhat self-conscious in such select company.

'Why did you not come home, Quiddy,' asked Mary, 'and give us a chance of welcoming home the returned hero?'

'Hero, Mary?' queried Quiddy. 'Why, I hadn't the courage to return to my home in Parva, not in the sorry state I was in—me, who had set off with such high notions of doing things.'

Quiddy lapsed into silence, and presently Julia took up the story:

'He's the stupidest man,' she began. 'He just won't talk about himself, though he must have gone through hell, but it's useless to ask him anything. I had lost all sight or sound of him for more than a year, when I decided to call at his old lodge in Exeter to see if perchance they had any news of him. I chanced to run across Quiddy in the street hobbling towards the house with the help of two sticks, so changed he was that I scarcely knew him. After some persuasion I took him to the pictures, hoping to

cheer him up, for he seemed to have lost all interest in life. It
was not a success, for, would you believe it, he blandly informed
me he had decided to break off our engagement. I asked him,
did he no longer love me, and he replied he loved me too well to
impose a crippled burden on my shoulders. I was greatly dis-
tressed, and though I pleaded that nothing mattered so long as we
were together, he was stubborn and said I must forget all about
him, that his career was finished, and he was only fit for the
scrap heap. I returned to camp in tears, heart-broken at the
thought of losing Quiddy. I had recently been sent to do some
clerical work at a W.R.A.F. station and what I did next, being
desperate, was for Quiddy's sake. A few days later I was given a
government contract to type out for some new Air Force
buildings to a man whose name was William Bland. I addressed
the contract to William Brunt at his address in Exeter and he got
the contract, with several more to follow. Since then Quiddy has
done well in government work, and has a reputation for good
honest work, which evidently is more than can be said for his
wife.'

'Oh, I wouldn't say that,' remarked Mary defensively. 'After
all everything turned out for the best and I think it was very
brave of you to act as you did.'

'Well, thank goodness it is all over now, and when the
W.R.A.F. was demobilized in 1919, and Quiddy had again begun
to take an interest in being alive, we decided to get wed in the
summer following. Not but what I had almost to do the proposing
myself,' ended Julia with a toss of her curls.

'And what about yourself, Julie?' went on Mary. 'You
disappeared all of a sudden and must have had an adventurous
career, though we did occasionally hear from you.'

'Why, Mary love, I'd better explain as this seems the day of
public confession. I was only seventeen at the time, and a horrid
stuck-up creature as you well know, but I had taken a liking for
Quiddy ever since we acted together in that first stage play,
Entering Society. Remember it, Mary? I will never forget that
night and how Quiddy kissed me at the garden gate.'

'I suppose you think you were the only girl to be kissed at a garden gate that glorious evening,' broke in Val rudely, to be severely rebuked by his wife.

'Seems to me, Frank,' said Jonathan, 'our late curate started something that evening. But carry on, Julie, let's hear the worst of it.'

'Why, Daddy, you remember what a wicked, head-strong girl I was in those days. Well, believe it or not, I told Quiddy I loved him, but could not marry him because he was poor, uneducated and lacking in refinement!'

'So presumably Quiddy has not only improved in circumstances, but in good manners and deportment, eh?' said Frank Smith.

'Not a bit of it, sir,' retorted Julia with a smile. 'Quiddy's manners are deplorable! He is still the wild, uncultivated Quiddy who stole my heart away on those hectic nights in the hut.'

'Now that's strange,' broke in Quiddy's mother, speaking for the first time. 'I remember that night as plain as anything, how he came home in such a taking as never was and said he wanted to leave home to better hissel. I blamed Mr Smith here for putting ideas into his head.'

'There you were mistaken, Mother,' broke in Quiddy. 'Mr Smith knew nothing about it. Julie had said she could not marry me because I was poor and uneducated, so I left home vowing I would not return until I had overcome these disabilities.'

'What a lovely story of the boy who made good!' interposed Mrs Smith. And what now, Quiddy? Still continuing with your sculpture work?'

'As a hobby,' replied Quiddy. 'As you probably know, Julie's dad wishes me to join the partnership of the Quarry Company when we've got settled down.'

'Yes,' broke in Julia, who did most of the talking. 'Daddy finds it very lonesome living by himself, though he still has Jubby the groom, and Quiddy's mother calls every day to do the housework. Mary used to come over every day from the farm, but now she has two babies to look after, she cannot manage it.'

'I had hoped that George—sorry, I mean your dad and mam, Mary, would have been here this afternoon,' mused Jon Keppel.

'It's the babies, Grandad,' replied Mary. 'Mam and Dad insisted on giving them a party and introducing them to their little cousin Jonathan, saying Julie would have enough on her hands without a toddler clinging to her skirts.'

'Aye, grandads have their uses, I suppose,' grunted Jon.

'But Dad says he will be calling in before long for a game of whist.'

They found much to discuss at this happy house-warming besides idle chatter, and while the womenfolk were helping Julia to serve tea, Quiddy remarked to Frank Smith:

'Don't you find Parva greatly altered, sir? I can scarcely find my way about since coming home.'

'It certainly has altered,' was the reply, 'and I try to think it has altered for the better, but I miss that quiet little village I discovered so many years ago. I can see it all so plainly. You were a schoolboy then, driving the cows home for milking. You and the old roadman were the first persons we met in Parva—do you remember, Quiddy?'

'No, I don't remember that particular occasion, but I remember the roadman. I would hardly suppose him to be still living?'

'No, he married Mrs Humble at the shop some years ago, and both the dear old souls have now passed on.'

'I see old Jubby is still on the go and looking hale and hearty for a man of his years. D' yer know, I was always scared of old Jubby as a kid, and to tell the truth I am rather surprised to find him in this select company.'

'Well, I suppose Mr Keppel can best explain that,' replied Frank, and, turning to his host, remarked: 'Jonathan, here is Quiddy, inquiring into the mystery of your groom and general factotum.

'Why, it's a mystery to me, Frank. Another of Julie's antics, a sort of levelling down process she has in mind that all men are equal. If this game keeps on it will end with me sleeping in the bothy, while Jubby occupies my bedroom. But what think you about it, Jubby? You haven't opened your mouth all the afternoon, except to stuff food in it?'

Jubby being thus admonished replied: 'I ain't leaving my little nook over the saddle-room for nobody, unless you kicks me out, sir. It's hur, Miss Julie, wants me to wed wi' Mrs Brunt, Master Quiddy's mother and go and live at The Spital.'

Jonathan, seeing the surprised look on Quiddy's face, explained:

'The Spital Farm and the park adjoining had belonged to Squire Brookfield, who died some time during the war years, and willed the property to the parish council on condition that they turned the house into a home for aged and respectable married couples, at a modest rentage. Now the old squire's groom, who was a particular friend of Jubby and wished to show his gratitude for Jubby's help to him in the past, conceived the idea of himself wedding the late squire's cook, who suffers from wind and stomach troubles, if only his friend Jubby can find a wife to join him in the venture. Although Jubby has quite a pile of money put by, or perhaps because of it, he refused to play up—until our Julie came home and got wind of it, and immediately began negotiations.'

The conversation was interrupted by Julia inquiring: 'What are you menfolk talking about so earnestly? Some mischief afoot, I'll be bound, when we are not asked to join in.'

'My dear girl,' replied Jonathan, 'you are capable of joining in without asking, and all we were talking about was the latest developments in the history of Parva, for Quiddy's benefit.'

Mrs Smith now broke in to say: 'It has always intrigued me how Quiddy came by such an unusual name. I know his proper name is William, but why Quiddy?'

'Well, I think I can answer that one,' declared Quiddy's mother. 'He wer' my first-born, and it was Sarah Crabthorn who brought him into the world and charged a gowden sovereign for the job. Well, when our Billy heard of it he gives a look at the bairn, and says. "A quid, eh!' and though we christened him Willum, Dad allwis used to call him Quiddy and the name stuck.'

'Well, it's high time Mr Brunt was called William and became a respectable gentleman,' declared Mrs Smith.

'I am afraid he will never be respectable and will always be Quiddy,' declared Julia in a rather grand manner.

It can be said that the party kept on to a late hour and ended most harmoniously.

CHAPTER FOURTEEN

Retrospect

THERE is little more can be said of that charming spot known as Nettleworth Parva. Indeed the visitor to that once charming group of cottages would fail to find the place, for even the name Parva has disappeared under the subordinate title of New Nettleworth.

Most of the old family names have disappeared from the district, and the once well-known name of Keppel is no longer listed among the directorship of the Quarry Company, but in its place is the name of William Brunt, the famous sculptor. George and Mabel Western, who farmed Wheatlands as though they expected to live for ever, have passed away, leaving the farm to Valentine and Mary Keppel, who find life all too short for Father's slow and methodical methods. Agricultural science, fertilizers and the very latest in machinery are Val's stock-in-trade, all of which is enough to make old George turn in his grave.

The name of Robinson is no longer heard in farming circles, though after the old man died Miss Harriet and her mother kept the farm going for another year or so. It was after Edward Robinson died that the family lawyer, of the firm of Skinn and Blood, became interested in the farm. Rather, it should be said he became interested in Miss Harriet, the sole child and sole legatee of all portable goods and effects upon the death of her mother. Miss Harriet during her active days on the farm had always a slim waist line due to her constant bending over chicken coops and the daily search for eggs of the hen that laid astray, which often necessitated her climbing to the top of the straw stacks. It will be seen from this that Miss Harriet in her days of bloom was a spritely, athletic sort of person. Indeed she was always on the run, and the only times she rode out were for occasional jaunts with Father in the pony-tub. I mention this because I chanced across the lady recently in the town of Kingsmill and had difficulty in recognizing her as the same person. After the farm sale, and final disposal of goods and effects, the junior partner of Skinn and Blood had proposed to Miss Harriet, and surprisingly Miss Harriet had said 'Yes'. Presumably there would have been some previous love making, though so far as the suitor was concerned it was chiefly a business concern. Here was a desirable female, not too young and not too old, but with a worthwhile nest-egg saved from the poultry undertaking, along with other fiduciary interests relative to a sale of farm stock and machinery. They were married at the Trinity Church in Magna at Miss Harriet's request, after which Harriet seems to have lost her Nonconformist way of life and conformed to the ways of suburbia in the select regions of Kingsmill. Now that there were no stacks to climb, no chicken coops over which to bend, gone were that slender waist, the trim ankles and the slender neck, and instead of an occasional ride out in the buggy drawn by a pony Miss Harriet now rides in a richly cushioned limousine propelled by internal combustion. As a result of this Harriet has lost all her curves and sits back among her cushions like a sack of wheat pulse. Which shows how wrong are the young reformers who try to place us all on the same level, since there will always be those of the buggy class and those of the limousine, the former propelled by Shanks and the latter by cranks.

The mention of Robinson's farm brings to mind the career of one of Tushy Whysall's sons Bert who worked on the farm. We referred to him as being horse proud, and were pleased to see he was following agriculture instead of, like other youths who had returned from the war, carrying bricks on the new building sites. It seems that our prognostications were premature, for on marrying a sweet young girl of the village he found that twenty-five shillings per week was as nothing compared with the enormous pay the brick-carriers were taking home each week. So, though he still retained his strong affection for horses, he found a job on the building sites carrying eight seven pounds of bricks at a time up a ladder, a most hideous task to be kept up all day. However, it was not the brick carrying that affected George but a combination of several other factors. He found, for instance, that if the gang had to knock off for an hour because of rain an hour's pay was deducted from his pay packet, which often reduced his weekly income to that of an agricultural worker. That was not the worst of his drawbacks, for while they sheltered from the rain a gaming board known as the Crown and Anchor was introduced. According to George's idea on the law of averages he ought to have an occasional win himself, but somehow the owner of the board, who was also the shaker of the dice, always turned out to be the winner. Still, George hoped for the best. Another drawback to fortune was the fact of the firm paying out their workmen at Saturday noon on the site, which was near the Prince of Wales Hotel. Hence it was the custom for several of the men to call in for a refresher before proceeding home with their pay. Depending on the extent of their thirst the pay packet was considerably reduced before they arrived home, and sad to relate George's pay packet kept in line with those of his friends.

Then a strange thing happened. The landlord, Ernest Munday, had bought a new turn-out, a smart stepping pony, silver-plated harness, varnished tub, rubber-tyred, all standing spick and span in the inn yard. George and his mates could not but stop to admire, especially George with his love of horse flesh. He remarked to the landlord:

'I guess that has cost you a pretty penny, Ernest.'

'Oh, I don't know, Bert, lad, it's such silly b——s as thee who's paid for this,' Ernest replied.

Which remark put Bert quite off his beer. He turned on his heel and went home without a further word and with his wage intact. His pals laughed and said, 'He'll soon be back', but they were wrong, for Bert Whysall was never again seen in a public house. If you doubt the veracity of the story, ask Bert Whysall of Nettlethorpe how he started his business as carting contractor, and he will tell you it was through someone telling him the truth; and he will describe how he started carting bricks with one decrepit old horse and now has a stable of eight of the finest horses in the district. But then George was always horse proud from his youth up.

One thing that arose out of the late war was the great drive in afforestation. Our woodlands were being denuded in the war effort, and it became essential to the nation's economy that much replanting should be undertaken. The district, lying on the borders of the forest, has always been well wooded with oak, ash and beech trees, but this new attempt at afforestation is concerned exclusively with conifers. The reason for this is that the 'hardwoods' take a matter of one hundred years to come to maturity, whereas the conifers, being of more rapid growth, can be felled for use in a matter of fifty or sixty years. There is too a great demand for conifers at this present time, especially for the Scotch pine which is used in the building trade for scaffold poles and floorboards or sawn down the centre to make two sides of a thirty-foot ladder; conifers are also in great demand as pit-props underground. These new plantations that are now hemming us in bear no similarity to the old open woodlands where the oaks and beeches seem to have been planted haphazard with lots of space between the trees. These conifers, larch, spruce and fir, are planted in straight regimental lines and packed closely together, so that neither sunshine nor shower can penetrate the dense foliage. Consequently neither primroses nor bluebells are to be found under their massed coverage.

Let the hustlers and the jerry-builders keep their scaffold-pole conifers, but for me the hardwoods—the oak and ash and beech. There is something venerable and awe-inspiring about an oak that has flourished through half the span of English history. What an interesting speculation as we gaze on a mighty forest oak that it was maybe a sapling tree when Agincourt was fought, or that Robin Hood once sheltered under its branches. Of all vegetation our woodlands are the most ancient, the most comprehensive and the most adaptable, for no one whatever his trade, profession or calling can pass through life without touching wood in some shape or form in the course of his duties.

This is the day of 'ready mades', windows and doors made to order, instead of as with the old village craftsman made to measure. Worth more than a passing glance was the beauty of a well-built oak gate—not a machine-made article but one put together by the village joiner or estate carpenter. No nails were used, for nails are apt to split the wood, the bars of the gate being slotted into the mortices of the uprights, and instead of nails dowels of oaken pegs or nuts and bolts were used to hold the bars in place. In this machine age plentiful nails and an abundance of putty to hide the faulty work have ousted the perfect symmetry achieved by the village craftsman.

The visitor would look in vain for the old stone cottages in Parva, as for their accompanying pigsties, for both were considered as being detrimental to the public health. The removal of the pigsties in particular caused much confusion of thought among the owners thereof, for the powers that be condemned the sties as being too near the dwelling place, while the 'earth closet', which primitive hygiene had placed at the farthest end of the garden path in the interest of good health and decency, the public health authorities had brought forward not only nearer to the dwelling place but actually indoors under the name of water-closets. There is no accounting for taste in this New Age.

One last look at Nettleworth Parva. The old wooden hut that first brought light into Parva, and placed it on the map as it were, has now been replaced by a superb building in dressed stone. A pleasing feature is the façade supported by Doric columns, while on either side of the wide entrance stand two stone-carved figures. All this work has been executed by the quarry manager, William Brunt, and over the main entrance are carved the words: 'THE FRANK SMITH MEMORIAL HALL'.